A LOST WORLD WHERE THE PEOPLE ARE BLUE

A GALAXY, ALIVE
BOOK ONE

REY S MORFIN

i

Also by Rey S Morfin...

A Galaxy, Alive
A Lonely World Where The People Are Blue
A Planet That Longs To Forget
A Fleet That Hunts An Endling
A World Of Lost Souls—**Coming Soon**

Smoke Without Fire
Life At The End Of The Road

Shorts
Come And See

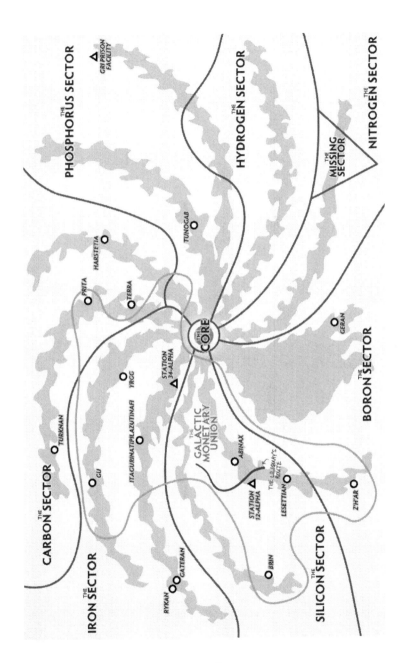

YRGG

THE PLANET OF DUST

Iron Sector

20a-11-2337

1. The Planet Yrgg Is Really Lovely At This Time Of Year

No matter where you go in the galaxy, you'll find that every planet has all the same issues as there are on Terra. Pride? Check. Wrath? Check. Envy? Check. Well, actually, the Guliens don't have that last problem, but there's definitely something weird going on in their wiring. Not that lacking envy is a bad thing, by any means; sometimes I wish I could be like them.

It's these very problems that pay for my lifestyle. Think your partner is cheating on you? Good chance they are. Got a missing child? They probably got sick of your crap and ran away. Convinced there's an intergalactic security organisation monitoring your every move because of your research into wormhole technology? Yeah... unlikely, mate, but I'll still gladly take your money.

Whatever it is, my agency can handle it. And, by "handle it", I mean they'll send me to go through the motions of solving the case, and then take their 70% share of the revenue without really contributing very much. Work is hard to come by, nowadays, much less well-paid work, so I take what I can get. Let's face it, it's rare that any single person gets to do anything particularly special with their lives. Certainly, most don't do anything to change the galaxy for the better, even if we aspire to it. Instead, we slave through our work each and every day, just trying to make sure we have enough Units to pay the bills.

It's on one of these mind-numbing—albeit bill-paying—jobs that our story begins.

_~v_

My assignment was a tall, beautiful Yrggian, who, according to her partner, was definitely, 100%, not an iota of doubt, cheating on him. Still, that didn't stop him from hiring my agency to make sure. These wealthy business types had more Units than they knew what to do with... not that I was complaining.

I had been following the target for several days, but she was yet to do anything out of the ordinary. There was no other special someone in her life, it seemed. All she really spent her time doing was going to work, going to the gym, and then seeing her friends for U'kka (where she would lie about going to the gym—she just naturally has this figure, she would say).

Normally, if there really was someone else in the target's life, I would have known by this point—rarely did they spend more than a few days at a time without getting their fill. That wouldn't stop me padding it out to a week or so in my reports, of course—I was paid by the hour, after all.

I watched from inside my parked Shuttle as the target left her home. She carried no gym bag, she wasn't scheduled for work, and she'd seen her mates just a few hours earlier in the day. This, _at last_, was her doing something new.

She pulled up her sleeve, revealing her Console, from which she summoned a shuttle. As she entered, I quickly programmed my own shuttle into manual overdrive. Without knowing where my target was going, I was going to have to drive it myself. For many, doing such a thing would have been unheard of—but in my profession it was necessary. Perhaps Private Investigators were the last remaining drivers in the galaxy.

Sure enough, the target led me to a new building—one that she hadn't been to before. I couldn't immediately determine its function; it looks like a corporate building, but as more and more Yrggian companies were merging, lots of these structures were being repurposed.

I jumped out of my parked shuttle while continuing to survey the building—and failed to immediately notice that the target had turned to glance at me over her shoulder. I began to walk away from her, in the other direction, hoping to throw her off the scent. The target shook her head and continued walking. Presumably, she was content that I *wasn't* following her—or about to mug her, or whatever—because she continued into the building. I thanked my lucky stars that she hadn't paid too much attention to me, and proceeded after her—at a distance—into the building.

There was no doorman in the lobby, but it didn't matter to the target—she knew exactly where she was going. But instead of moving to the inter-level transmat, she proceeded down the stairs, to the basement.

Exactly what kind of kinky shit was this woman in to?

I continued after her, stopping at every corner to carefully look around before I followed. Being seen twice by a target was never good. I knew this from experience; on one of my first cases, my target—a lonely Pritan—had caught me watching him a few times, and had called the local police. That was not a good day for me.

The Yrggian turned into a room. Creeping forwards, and then

crouching at the doorway, I peered in.

It was a large hall, with a ring of chairs at the centre. In the corner, there were cheap baked goods carefully positioned on an old table. There was the unmistakable vibe of polite enthusiasm and in the room. It was one of *these* sorts of meetings, then; the kind that my mother used to go.

Stirliks Anonymous.

The group inside said their "hello"s, their "how you doing"s, and their "how's the partner"s, before the conversation eventually turned serious. I needed to get closer so I could get clear evidence of this meeting for my client. He'd need proof, after all.

Even by my standards, it felt like a breach of privacy to take a photograph of someone at one of these meetings. I could picture myself reacting to the hypothetical news that my mother's meeting had been intruded upon in this same way. Nothing in the galaxy would be able to calm me down. Nothing, except perhaps cupcakes. Or whiskey.

The attendees sat uncomfortably in their seats, picking nervously at themselves, barely making eye contact with one another. Most were positioned so that they were most of the way off their chair—and most of their way towards the door.

Mum had started using the 'Liks after Dad left. Something had changed in her in those last few months. My youthful self was perhaps unable to perceive exactly what was plaguing her. Whatever it was, she took the 'Liks to forget. That was what they did, of course: they took in old memories—the bad ones—and wiped them from your mind. Why live a miserable life when you could live a joyful one?

It didn't matter to these addicts too much that it wasn't real. Whatever it was that Mum had experienced to drive her to this, we would never know—her memories of the period were no longer a reflection of reality.

I'd been about eight and my sister, Leya, fourteen. It had really been Leya who had run the household for those few years; trauma like this had a habit of making adults out of children. I had always intended to thank Leya for all she did for me back then, but as I watched her walk out that door that final time, the words were lost from my mouth.

I needed to see Mum. It had been too long. I was getting lazy with how often I went back to Terra. I plugged this in as a reminder on my console, and set my eyes on the job at hand, and getting closer to the group.

Spotting a strategically-placed bench to my left, I slowly, silently, crept towards it.

'Please welcome, new member: Syl Raynor,' an automated female Yrggian voice announced.

Hmm. OK. Not ideal.

The group all turned in their chairs to look at me, crouched down in the corner of the room.

'...Hi,' I offered them.

'Welcome, welcome!' a particularly jolly Aflet called out to me. He was the organiser, then. 'Come on in, don't be shy!'

I looked at the door; it was still open. I could still turn around and walk through it... but I would lose my opportunity to solve this case. I rose timidly into a standing position and proceeded towards the group.

My target, eyes widening as she looked at me, stood up and pointed. 'It's you!' she shouted. Then, looking at the organiser, added, 'She's the one that's been following me! She's been stalking me!'

OK, maybe outside this building wasn't the first time she'd seen me, then. My agency really needed to send me on more training courses. Always the Terran who got passed over for them, wasn't it?

One of the attendees, sitting with their back to me, pounded a fist onto his knee. He stood from his seat, rising to a height of maybe two and a half metres. Not a little lad, by any means. Slowly, he turned to face me, and I could see the anger on his face—the nostrils flaring, the brow furrowed. The host held out his hands in instruction—or perhaps in appeal—for the Yrggian to remain calm.

'Now, what do we do when we feel these negative emotions?' he prompted. There was no reply from the tall, broad, attendee staring me down.

'That's right,' the host continued, even though nobody had said anything, 'We communicate how we *feel!* Can we try that now?'

'You *dare,*' the Yrggian began, voice raised, 'Interrupt one of these meetings? Is *nothing* sacred any more?'

He pointed at my target.

'This poor woman has been through *enough!* She does *not* need you following her, giving her more to worry about. What the *hell* do you think gives you the right to barge in here?'

All signs suggested that my time in this room was about to come to an end. I whipped out my headpiece from my satchel, and without even bothering to put it on my head, aimed it in the direction of the target to capture her image.

Most of the group simply stared at me, faces pulled in various states of incredulity; it was only the Yrggian that took action. Face going red—even for an Yrggian—he began to plough towards me. With my height being as it were, it was almost certainly clear to anyone in the vicinity that this was a fight I would lose—were we to count on strength alone. I rolled up my right sleeve, revealing a device on my wrist, and grinned slyly as I switched it on. The EMP whirled into action, letting out a wave of radiation, and the lights went out.

'Ahaha, see you later, motherfli-,' I began.

'Backup lighting activated,' the automated voice announced—and once again I was in plain sight.

'Dang,' I uttered through pursed lips, 'I'm really starting to hate her.'

The enraged Yrggian barrelled towards me, grabbed me by the clothes and hoisted me up effortlessly.

Now dangling, and unable to pull myself free, I asked my assailant, 'You wouldn't hit a woman, would you?'

He looked at me, eye narrowing, eyebrow raised. 'You are a *female* of your species?'

I scoffed, pulled an overtly unimpressed face at him. 'Woah, what's that supposed to mean, mate? *Rude.*'

In one smooth flick of my left wrist, I whipped out my hidden blade and held it to the Yrggian's throat.

'What we gonna do now, then?' I asked him.

He looked at me, his forehead clenching involuntarily, in that way Yrggians do when they're thinking too hard.

Eventually, he released me, and I tumbled clumsily to the floor, landing on my arse.

As I scrambled backwards for the door, the broad Yrggian called after me. 'We have your name, Syl Raynor!'

I fled the scene, trying to suppress the guilt that was blossoming in the pit of my stomach. It maybe hadn't been my finest hour.

~

I entered my shuttle and activated the pre-programmed route back to my hotel. I watched my rear keenly for the next few minutes, and only once I was confident that nobody was following me did I send off the images to the client.

Soon, I got a reply from him, telling me that my contract was fulfilled and that the payment would be sent to my employers.

No tip, then. Damn. What was it with these posh types and not tipping?

It didn't matter, at least the job was complete. I could now head to a local bar, relax, try out the Yrggian brandy which I'd heard so much about. I freshened up and was about to head out— when my Console beeped.

There was a new message... from the agency. My heart dropped; this wasn't expected, and so the likelihood was that it wouldn't be good.

'What the *hell* is this?' the message began. I skimmed the remainder of it, getting the general point: they were annoyed with me. At the bottom, I found an attachment.

Beneath a security image of me, taken in the basement where the meeting had been held, was a message in bold, red letters:

Wanted for questioning: Syl Raynor.

It was time to get off this planet for a while.

TERRA

THE MENDED WORLD
Carbon Sector
22-11-2337

WEMBLEY CITY

THE EALING CENTRE

THE GREAT WILLESDEN ESTATES

RICHMOND PARK REFUGEE CAMP

WIMBLEDON ISLANDS

BUCKINGHAM PALACE

HAMPSTEAD TOWERS

HERE BE CROYDON

THE SOHO MARSHLANDS

THE THAMES DELTA

STREATHAM SHIPYARD

STREATHAM ISLAND

HERNE DOCKYARDS

THE CRYSTAL PALACE

LEWISHAM BAY

THE BROMLEY TECHLANDS

WOOLWICH PENINSULA

12

2. Home Is Where The Nightmares Are

The transport ship glided down around the Crystal Palace, a tall glass spire piercing the heavens, with the EEO neon sign standing proudly towards the top. I watched the waves lick at Streatham Island's flood defences as the ship queued to dock at the local shipyard.

This city had changed a hell of a lot over the past few hundred years. Until the mid-2100s, London was one of the largest capitals in the world. Of course, the Climate Crisis soon put an end to that, with large swathes of city being taken over by the sea. It wasn't just in the continent of Europa, either. The capital of the Americas, Rio de Janeiro, was completely wiped off the map, with locals being relocated to the higher lands of Brasilia.

Where the Americas still had empty space, Europa did not. It had already grown hugely overpopulated by the time of the Climate Crisis, and so there was no land left on which to relocate anyone. Instead, we built upwards—towering structures pierced the skyline, and none peaked higher than the third Crystal Palace.

A long, winding bridge protruded from the northwestern-most point of Streatham Island, connecting the north side of what used to be London to the remaining strongholds in the south. This bridge snaked around the heavily-fortified Buckingham Palace, which was abandoned long ago, even before the last days of the monarchy. Then, it proceeded to the southernmost tip of the Great Willesden Estates, skirting around the now-uninhabitable Soho Marshlands.

'Marshlands' was an informal name, of course. There was nothing particularly marshy about Soho nowadays, except perhaps for the high water level. Instead of tall reeds and fine grasses, it was rubble that sprouted from the water—bricks, metal and the like.

We finally touched down at the Streatham Shipyard, and I joined another long queue: customs. It was almost laughable, the idea that a Terran might try to smuggle something into the planet. No Terran I'd ever known would have been capable of breaking the law in such an overt manner. How would they reconcile that with themselves? In fact, the worse I had ever seen a Terran do was drive their shuttle through a yellow light—and that was enough to elicit audible gasps from everyone in the vicinity. Full disclosure: *I* was that Terran.

It was visitors, I supposed, that the Terran government was concerned about. Who knows what such *immoral* species might bring on to their wonderful (if half-destroyed) planet? But they couldn't just wave the Terrans through, of course. Treating species differently like that would have caused international outrage. Understandable, really. So we had to suffer through it in silence.

I brought up my console while I was in the queue, gave my mother an estimated time of arrival. She read the message and sent no reply. Typical. Or maybe she was just busy.

I'll give you the benefit of the doubt this time, Mum.

When I eventually got through the shipyard security, I

summoned a shuttle from my console, threw my lightly-packed bag in the back, and programmed in my mum's address. This was the last time I would see this place, I noted; she was moving home tomorrow. I thought of those younger years spent in that home, in that cramped, dim space, and of staring out the windows that faced only other apartment blocks. It held a special place in the heart that was reserved only for a childhood home.

The shuttle wound through the overly-complicated shipyard transport network, until, finally, it brought me out on to the main road heading north. My Mum's place—my Mum's *old* place, I began to condition myself—wasn't far from the shipyard, just a few miles north. This would be the last time I would have such an easy journey. The transport network around the Woolwich Peninsula, on the other hand, was nowhere near as smooth—not that anyone on Terra would be so negative as to admit such a flaw.

I exited the shuttle outside the block of flats that had paid host to my childhood home, and I looked up at it, taking it in one last time. Every few floors were painted a separate colour, each relating to a certain profession. The idea had been that neighbours who worked in the same industries would have more in common, and it would make for a more civilised living arrangement. This was classic 2290s New Age nonsense.

I took the transmat to the thirty-first floor (which was a pale fuschia, signifying that artists lived there), and the front door sensor alerted my mother to my presence. The door, recognising me as a trusted user, opened automatically, revealing my mum crouching beside a pile of hovering metal crates.

'Syl! You're here!' she called out, acting surprised, as though her Home System hadn't already told her this.

'Yeah, I'm here, Mum. How are you?'

'I'm good sweetheart, I'm good,' she replied, wrapping her arms around me. 'And how is my little girl?'

'I'm twenty-four, Mum. This "little girl" business has to stop at some point.'

'Oh,' she replied, waving dismissively at me, 'Let me have that one.'

I looked around at the apartment, which was still, largely, unpacked.

'I see it's going... well,' I said.

'I know, I know! I'm behind. What's new? That's what you're here for, though, isn't it? To help?'

I resisted the urge to roll my eyes. 'Yes, mother. Can I at least get a cup of tea first?'

Mum asked the house for two cups, and the machines in the kitchen whirred into life. In my youth, the equipment had been new, operating silently but for a soft purr. Now, after years upon years of use, the gears in the machines were beginning to grind, the pipes were slightly clogged, and, to be honest, it could all have done with being ripped out and replaced. But we don't do that, not on Terra, not any more.

'So how have you been? Really?' I asked.

She shrugged. 'I don't want to say things have been hard. I mean, we live on *Terra* after all. It's not like there's anywhere better out there.'

'You'd be surprised, Mum.'

'Maybe there's places for *you*, Syl, but not for an old girl like me. Terra's the only place I've known... it's too late for me to start anywhere new. Right now, though, this just doesn't feel like home.'

'Turknan is supposed to be nice at the moment? Since the droughts ended.'

Mum shook her head. This was a pointless exercise, it seemed.

'Is this anything to do with the move?' I asked.

She looked me in the eyes, a pained expression on her face,

and nodded. 'There's just no work for me, here, not any more. The whole floor is moving—art isn't important to Terra like it used to be. Government's preoccupied with standard of living, but what's the point of living in a world without the arts?'

'I know, Mum, I know...'

'It was that...,' she paused, bent towards me conspiratorially, her hand partially covering her mouth, and whispered a word I'd never heard her say before. '...*bloody* GMU business, wasn't it?'

'Woah, Mum, no need to swear like that!' I responded, in both jest and horror that my own mother would use a word like 'bloody'.

'I'm sorry, Syl, I'm just so wound up by it all. Didn't know I'd lose my home, did I? Thought leaving the GMU was just about preserving our culture, it wasn't like they explained all the nitty-gritty trade details to us. Not like I knew that Terran arts were propped up by GMU subsidies...'

She shook her head, forced a smile, and continued, 'Sorry. You don't want to hear about something as boring as trade agreements when there's a whole galaxy of adventures out there, do you?'

'No, Mum, it's OK, honest. I get it. I'm sad to lose this place too.'

'The new place will be nice, too, though,' she replied, her voice wobbling in that way it did when she was lying to herself.

'Have you seen it?'

'Yeah. Set up the transmitter there yesterday.'

'You got a transmitter? Very posh!' I said, encouragingly.

'Comes as standard with state-provided housing, don't you know! Saves you loading all your stuff in a shuttle, which, let's face it, is the worst thing about moving.'

When I needed a break from my mother, as all daughters often do, I offered to start packing in the study. My mum, grateful for any help that I could give her, told me to have at it.

I remembered Dad using the study a lot. It was one of the few memories I had of him. He would position himself in the corner of the room, in a large armchair, sat facing the very left-hand side of the window, where you could see a small slither of the view to the south. I never knew what he was pondering so deeply, but even then, I could tell from his body language that it was important.

Nowadays, Mum had set up shop in there for her art. A huge digital tablet, her pride and joy (even more so than me) sat on an antique wooden easel.

Now, you have to be careful with this, Syl, it's very old, from the twenty-second century. Do you know how long ago that was? That was over a hundred years ago! You'll be careful, now, won't you?

Yes, Mum!

I trod slowly about the easel, heading first for the desk in the corner of the room. Mum kept it tidy—really, she had little need to use it—and so I was surprised when I found an old journal in the drawer.

I pulled the diary from the desk and fumbled for the on-switch on the top. It whirred into life, and I was shocked when I read the lock screen.

Diary of Leya Raynor, 2331 to 2336.

I remembered the moment Mum had rung me, back in early '32. I remembered the tears when she'd told me that Leya was missing; both hers and mine. I remembered us agreeing that we would do our bests to find her.

And yet, this journal was here. How could this have been? How could-

'Mum?!' I shouted. 'What on *Terra* is this?'

When my mother poked her head around the corner, her face soon dropped. She lunged towards me, meaning to grab at the journal, but I pulled it away from her.

'You have Leya's diary? From while she's been missing? And you didn't tell me?!'

'I knew if I told you, you'd want to take it. And didn't want you losing it.'

'I'd lose it? What are you talking about?'

'Well, you know... since you started drinking you haven't exactly had your life completely in order, have you?'

'Mum! You can't say something like that to your daughter! Not like you don't have your *own* vices, is it? And to keep something like *this* from me?'

I paused, realising that maybe I'd gone too far by referring to her Stirlik addiction. 'What does... what does it say?!'

She shrugged.

'I don't know. I've tried decoding it. I've taken it to every specialist on Terra, but... nothing.'

'Can I try?' I asked.

Mum looked at me with sad eyes. 'I... she sent it to *me...*'

I could see that this diary meant more to my mother than I had realised. It was her last remaining memento of my sister, and I could see the parallels with her losing the journal, too.

'Please...,' Mum continued, holding out her hand.

Repressing both sadness and irritation, I gave the diary to her. She held it to her chest, close to her heart.

'You could have told me you had it.'

'And you wouldn't have tried to take it from me?'

I said nothing; we both knew the answer to that.

'I need some air,' I said suddenly, surprising even myself.

I took the transmat down to the ground floor and allowed myself to walk around the area one last time.

Like everywhere on Terra, the streets were pristine. So clean were they, in fact, that I could see that their spotlessness even in the dark of the evening light. Long had issues like littering been eradicated and the cleaning process itself perfected.

Where once my mother's street had been full of art galleries, restaurants, bars, there was now nothing. All commercial enterprises had been placed by more residential properties. The charm that this area once had was now gone.

It was the lack of bars that particularly frustrated me.

A Terran man turned the corner in front of me, heading towards me. I waved him down as he grew closer.

'Hey, do you know where the nearest bar is around here? I used to go to the Woodsman, but…'

'The Woodsman?' he replied. 'That's not been around for a few years now. You want a drink, you're better off heading to the main road.'

The main road was a good half-hour walk away. I hadn't been expecting my search for a drink to require so much physical exertion.

'Thanks,' I told the man, letting him go… and then I called after him again. 'Hey, do you work 'round here?'

The man shook his head. 'Not any more.'

'What were you, a waiter, barman?'

'Something like that. Why'd you ask?'

'Where do you work now?' I grilled him, completely ignoring his own question.

'EEO. Ethics Export Office. Down at the Crystal Palace.'

I pursed my lips. 'Yeah, I know what it stands for.'

The man smiled at me. 'I suppose everyone does.'

With that, he turned away from me and continued on with his life without me in it.

My quest for a drink turning out to be unexpectedly convoluted, I instead turned back, heading for my childhood home.

When I returned, Mum was already asleep. I poked my head into her bedroom—to see Leya's diary sitting on the pillow next to her.

I resisted my very un-Terran instinct to steal it from her while she slept.

Instead, I went to Leya and I's childhood room, which was preserved exactly as it had been when we'd lived here, and fell straight to sleep.

I awoke in the night to screams.

This wasn't the first time this had happened in this apartment. During my childhood, I'd often be rudely awoken in the night by the sound of a woman shrieking. Always, the source was my mother.

I rushed to her room to find her sitting bolt upright in bed, slowly coming back to the land of the conscious.

My Mum looked up to see me standing in the doorway.

'It's OK,' she reassured me, 'It's OK.'

I sat down on the bed next to her. 'I think I'm the one who is supposed to be saying that to *you*.'

Mum laughed gently—that kind of laugh where you breathe ever so slightly harder than normal out of your nostrils. Clearly her heart wasn't in it.

'I thought you weren't having these nightmares any more. Not since...'

I trailed off, but Mum finished the sentence for me.

'Not since the 'Liks. It's OK, you can say it.'

'I mean... yeah. I thought whatever memory was causing these nightmares, they'd overwritten.'

'Once upon a time that was true. But one of them has been coming back to me. Over and over, every night.'

21

'For how long?' I asked.

'Months now. Three... maybe four.'

'Mum...,' I began. 'You could've told me.'

'Oh, I didn't want to worry you. I know you have lots on your plate already with that job you have.'

'What is it? The memory?'

'I don't know if I should say, Syl. Some things you're better off not knowing.'

'First the journal, now this. Mum, you can't protect me forever. I'm not that little girl you still seem to think of me as.'

My mother paused, looked at me for a moment as she processed this information.

'I know,' she said at last, 'You're right.'

'Tell me.'

'I don't know if you'd believe me.'

'Trust me, I believe all kinds of things.'

'It's about your father. I...'

She trailed off. I prompted her to continue.

'Go on.'

'I remember him... controlling Leya. I don't mean verbally. Or even physically. But like... a puppet master might control a puppet. Or a brain might control its body. But it wasn't his body, it was her's.'

'You're talking about telepathy. Telepathy doesn't exist, Mum. It's a myth. We've known this for decades.'

Mum looked at me, tears in her eyes. 'I knew you wouldn't believe me.'

I felt my gut wrench in the way that only disappointing a parent can make happen. 'Sorry. I believe you. Go on.'

'I would've thought I was imagining it, too. But Leya... before she left, she told me, she remembers it happening to her. It was innocent things at first, like stopping crying fits, but then it got more sinister. He stopped her from going out, from having friends, until all her free time was spent in the house. Here. With him.'

'How...,' I began, not quite sure if I wanted to hear the answer to the question I was about to ask. 'How does she remember this? Wouldn't she have been a bit young?'

Mum burst out in tears. 'I'm sorry! I'm sorry! I should have stopped him sooner!'

'It was me, too, wasn't it?'

Mum forced the sobs to stop, and nodded, her eyes red. 'You were too young to remember, Syl. But Leya... she wasn't. She has to live with it.'

'And you think these are the memories you overwrote with the 'Liks?'

'Yes. Well, some of them, at least. But how can I know for sure what I've erased from my mind?'

This was getting all too much to process.

'So... you made Dad leave? Because of this?'

'I...,' Mum began to reply through sobs, 'I think so.'

'Mum, this is...'

I trailed off, and we sat in silence for a while, processing everything that had been said.

Eventually, Mum piped up again. 'There's something else...'

I looked at her with wide eyes, afraid to ask the necessary question.

'What else?'

'Leya, when she left... She told me she was going to go looking for him. Get answers about what he did to her. And to you.'

I touched at my cheek and found that it was wet. I'd been crying.

'She went looking for him?'

Mum nodded.

'You need to give me that journal, Mum. I need to find out where she went. You can't protect me from this any more.'

She nodded again, still remaining silent, but reached for the diary—and passed it to me.

I took it and stared blankly into the distance for a few moments.

'You'll tell me what you find, won't you?' Mum asked. 'I promise I won't use again. I'll live with the truth this time.'

'When I find anything, I'll tell you,' I lied.

The console on my arm began to vibrate. It was the agency again:

Holiday's over. We need you in. ASAP.

STATION 34-ALPHA

$$\overline{34\alpha}$$
$$\dagger$$

"NEXT SERVICES: 7.5 BILLION KILOMETRES"
Iron Sector
25c-11-2337

3. Not Bad For A Terran

I spent the journey flipping through the encrypted pages of Leya's journal, to no avail. Not only did I not see any way of easily decoding it, but I barely recognised some of the languages being used. It was split into sections—which I could only assume were ordered chronologically—each using a different set of characters. Beaten by this puzzle, I slammed the book shut and returned to staring absent-mindedly out the ship window.

When I docked back at Station 34-Alpha, I was welcomed with the familiar hustle and bustle of the central promenade. Businesses lined the Strip—a great many of them owned by fine, upstanding members of our great galaxy. There was a Gulian restaurant that served food which would fill you up as quickly as you wished—a single bite for those in a hurry, or several courses for those travelling for leisure. A bar, manned by a mute Iyr who never seemed to remove his helmet, sold some of the purest alcohol on the galaxy—just don't expect great service. And who could talk of 34-Alpha without mentioning the great Trunon, the best plasma-spinner in the sector?

Other businesses, such as the one I worked for, were not held in quite so much high regard. The shopfront was coated in a thick layer of dust, the door's opening protocol needed fixing up, and the ageing holosign was more often than not hacked to instead display pornography (courtesy of the kids of the promenade). These three issues conspired to give the agency the illusion of being a strip club and attracted all the wrong sorts of customers.

As I entered the agency premises, a small, rotund Bringla looked up from his desk. Well, *mostly* he did—two of his eyes remained trained on his console. Typically he would be sat, locked up, in his office, but today he was using the communal desks, perhaps taking advantage of nobody else being around.

'Raynor. You're late. Expected you back here two rotations ago,' he started.

'Yes, sir. Sorry. Came from Terra, other side of the sector. Traffic was a nightmare.'

'Ah... yes. I forget that you're one of *those*. From Terra. Maybe keep that hush-hush for the time being, eh?'

'What? Why? What's going on?'

'You mean to say you haven't figured it out yet? What sort of detective are you? Come on, Raynor. I'm sat out here, my office door closed, what do you *think* is going on?'

Oh, leave it out, mate, I'm tired.

'Maybe, *sir*, if you sent me on those training programmes you promised when I signed on at this agency, I'd have worked it out.'

Hutch sighed and rolled a few eyes in exasperation.

'Well, good news and bad. Good news is the company's been purchased, everyone with shares gets a payout.'

'I don't have shares.'

'Oh? Really? Shit. Just bad news for you, then. You have a new boss. He's been waiting for you. Everyone else has come and gone.'

Hutch nodded to the closed office door. I noticed that his name had been programmed out of the nameplate, replaced by the name of a P Saotchun.

My former boss nodded at me. 'Yes, go on. Don't keep him waiting any longer than you have to.'

What's the worst that could happen? They fire me? Maybe I should get out of this hellhole anyway.

I walked, cautiously, up to the office door and poked my head around it.

'Mr Saotchun?'

Another Bringla sat at Hutch's old desk. He, too, was small and rotund. Maybe they were just all like that; I couldn't remember ever meeting a Bringla before Hutch.

'Ah, you must be Ms Raynor, is that right?'

Without waiting for an answer, he brought my file up on the holoscreen in front of him.

I sat down on the chair opposite and opened my mouth to speak. In response, Saotchun put his hand up to my face, signalling that he needed longer to read my file.

If I'm as late as Hutch seems to think I am, couldn't he have read it in the meantime?

I analysed his face as he continued to read. If this Bringla's facial cues were the same as Hutch's, then he was getting less and less impressed the more he read. I hoped that I was wrong.

Eventually, he began to speak. 'So I assume Hutch filled you in outside?'

'Not really. Only that you'd bought the company.'

'That's right. And, like any business-savvy individual would when taking over a new company, I began with performance reviews. I'm happy to say that over sixty percent of your colleagues passed with flying colours!'

Nice!

'...The others will be fired.'

Oh.

'Well,' I began, a smile on my face, 'I look forward to working together!'

The Bringla looked me in the eyes for the first time since I entered his office.

'Oh, you assume you have passed, do you?'

'No, no, I don't mean that. I just mean... I was just being polite.'

'Hmm.'

The room fell silent again for a few more moments.

'Your performance reports do not impress.'

'Well, I'm fairly new here, and I haven't had much in the way of the training that was promised yet, and-'

'So you're blaming the lack of training for these average results?'

'Well, I- Wait, average? I thought you said my performance was bad?'

The Bringla seemed to tut at me. *Bringla don't tut, do they?*

'*No*, I said your performance "does not impress". I like to pride myself on only employing investigators who *exceed* expectation. You do not. At least, you don't by my usual standards. But it says here... you're a Terran?'

'Did my stunning good looks not give it away?' I asked, and then immediately regretted this flippant response. Sometimes I just couldn't resist saying these things.

'They did not, no,' Saotchun replied, giving me a funny look. 'If I were to judge you against my usual standards, I would fire you straight away, but...'

He trailed off, and I couldn't help but wonder if this was just for dramatic effect. I remained silent, waiting for him to finish his train of thought.

'Can you say "fuck" yet?'

I raised an eyebrow. 'I'm sorry?'

'This word: fuck. I met another Terran once, he refused to say it. He was insistent that to use such a word would go against everything that he, and all Terrans, hold dear: their morals.'

'I mean...,' I replied, 'I could say it if you really want...'

I could picture my mum shouting at me, horrified that I would say such a thing.

Young woman, you wash that mouth out this minute, you hear me?

'Can you?' Saotchun replied. 'That's not a rhetorical question, I stress. You see, all the Terrans I've met have been missing that certain... quality. That edge, that investigators need in order to do their jobs well. That ability to bend the rules, to break them if they see fit. I've never known a Terran to do that. In fact, they go the other way: they look to spread their sense of morality amongst the stars. I've never known a race without religion to be so preachy. So, with this in mind, I ask you: will you say it?'

'Yes, I can say it.'

'Well, then...'

A pause. Only by giving in could I fill the empty air.

'F... fuck.'

Saotchun roared with laughter, clapped some of his hands together with joy.

'I wish I'd recorded that. A Terran, swearing? Who would've thought it!'

He waved his hand over the desk communicator, opening a line to the outside office.

'Hutch, come in here, will you? And bring the last file.'

After a scuffling from outside, the door opened behind me, and Hutch stood at the threshold to the room, file in hand.

'Did she pass?' he asked, mouth hanging slightly open.

Well don't look so surprised, mate.

'She's on probation,' Saotchun replied. 'Give her the file, will you?'

Hutch ambled on over, placed the tablet on the desk in front of me.

'This case,' the new boss told me, 'Will either cement you as a permanent member of the team, or it will be your last case. You understand?'

I nodded.

'Now, unfortunately, I let all the employees who arrived back here *on time* choose their own cases, and so this one... this one is the case nobody picked.'

I looked down at the file in front of me. It was a missing persons case. Of course it was—my colleagues were no fools.

'So I-' I began to ask, before I was interrupted by Saotchun.

'So if you solve this case, you stay on the team, yes.'

'But it's a missing persons case! We solve maybe... one in ten of these.'

'Well, then,' the Bringla replied, an overtly fake grin on his face, 'Maybe you'll arrive on time for your next performance review?'

I nodded, looked down at the console, and skimmed through it.

'Missing daughter... government minister...'

'Yes, very sharp man, he was,' Saotchun added. 'An Itagurina... Itagurinato... Itagurinatipi...'

'Itagurinatipilaz,' Hutch offered.

'Yes! One of them. They're a very sharp species, aren't they? You Terrans could learn a thing or two from them! Anyway, yes: missing daughter of a government minister. Last seen on Z'h'ar, amongst the...'

Saotchun's eyes scanned the document. '...Amongst the Iyr— oh, that's an easier one!'

As I skimmed, I saw something else on the page, which made my heart drop.

31

'It says here this is a "no win, no fee" kinda case? How do you expect to turn a profit with that clause in our contracts?'

Saotchun laughed. 'Well, Ms Raynor, I expect us to turn a profit by having employees skilled enough to solve these cases. And that's precisely why some of your colleagues had to go.'

He shot Hutch a damning look, and my old boss suddenly became very interested in his shoes.

'Look, it's not just me, or my colleagues—nobody solves these kinds of cases. Nobody! Usually, by the time we even *receive* these cases, the target is long gone, off-planet, maybe even dead. You're really gonna give me this as the only chance to save my job?'

'I am, yes.' He leant in close. 'Look, don't get me wrong, I've been in your position before. I didn't inherit my managerial title; I worked for it, and, at the very start of my career, I, too, was the latest recruit in some crappy agency which barely turned a profit.'

Hutch opened his mouth as if to argue this point, but then thought better of it.

'But you know what I did?' he asked me.

'What?'

'I worked. Hard.' Saotchun sat back in his seat, no longer pretending to be sharing some big, dark, secret with me. 'And I solved cases like this. And then I got promotions, and I learned to manage people, to delegate. And, after a great many years of hard work, I now own a chain of detective agencies throughout the sector. I am living my dream. So, if I were you, I would work hard, solve this case, and think about where you want to be in five cycles.'

Saotchun stood up from his desk and opened the door for me to leave.

'Solve this, or you're out, understand?'

I nodded.

'Good. I'll be keeping three of my eyes on you.'

Z'H'AR

THE LONELY WORLD
Boron Sector
27f-11-2337

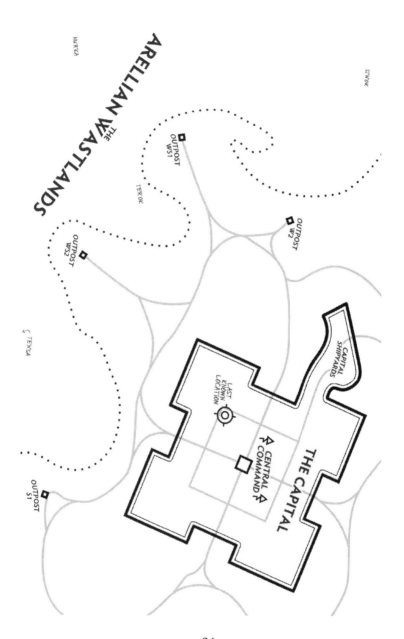

34

4. A Cold, Quiet, and Lonely Type of Folk

The planet Z'h'ar turned out to be halfway across the galaxy from Station 34-Alpha. Of course it was; this was the sort of luck I was having nowadays. While I had heard of Z'h'ar, I didn't know much about it—because it didn't exactly impact much on my day-to-day life. Being the responsible employee that I was, I spent the journey reading up on my destination.

Z'h'ar was populated by two intelligent species, but to group both into that same category was kinda disingenuous.

One species, the Iyr, were an advanced people, key members of the GMU, and known particularly for their head-to-toe mechsuits. These suits were installed with a number of programmes giving the user incredible new abilities. They might provide extra strength, night vision, in-built virtual assistants—you name it, they had it. Of course, not every Iyr would have every function included in their suit—such abilities were expensive—and typically only owned programmes relevant to their employment. Most notably of all—or so the guidepage would have had you believe—nobody outside of their race had ever seen the face of an Iyr.

The other supposedly intelligent species, the Arellians, were little more than barbarians—the equivalent of Terrans over two thousand years ago. They were a rural civilization—as such, they tended to keep to themselves, farm the land, and were barely even aware of the existence of people from other planets. As a result, little was known about their species.

I stared at the planet as we approached, wondering to myself how on Terra I was going to solve this likely unsolvable case, on this planet I had never before visited. It was, if nothing else, a long shot.

I suppose I could go work in a bar somewhere. I've always fancied doing something like that. Maybe I'd be happier there, anyway. No travelling involved, of course, but at least I could count on regular tips.

We touched down and I was greeted by a rather cold customs official. There were none of the smiles of home, only a long stare up and down, and a look that seemed to say "what on Z'h'ar are you doing here?" ...but it was hard to tell exactly what expression they were pulling from under that helmet.

'I see you left this part of the form blank,' the border guard said, pointing at the visa application. 'Referring to where you will be staying on your visit?'

'Ah, yes,' I replied. 'It was kinda a last-minute thing, so I don't have anywhere yet, but I'll be staying at a hotel in town, I guess.'

'I can't let you through until you have somewhere to stay.'

'But I-'

'I can't let you through until you have somewhere to stay,' the guard repeated, their tone exactly the same as the first time around.

I shook my head in exasperation, tapped in 'Z'h'ar hotels' on my console and booked the first one that came up. It took a whole five seconds to do. Maybe I could have found a better price if I had browsed for a little while, but I was too petty to pass up on an opportunity to be passive-aggressive.

'There,' I replied, showing the guard the confirmation page, 'Ut'r'a hostel, Central Stronghold.'

The guard nodded, waved me through, and shouted, 'Next!' to the queue behind me.

I passed through security and summoned a shuttle from my console. Before I could jump in it, a larger Iyr pushed in front of me, chucking their luggage into the back.

'Hey, that one's mine!' I called out to the Iyr.

The only response I was given was a mildly-irritated grunt. They closed the door and I was forced to summon another. That was a whole thirty seconds of my time wasted already. Not that half a minute was going to make the difference between me finding this girl and not.

After checking in to the hotel (and, of course, spending a good quarter of an hour simply lying on the bed, staring up at the ceiling), I headed out to the target's last known location. There was no time like the present—especially when my job was on the line.

My best chances, really, were in the target returning home by herself. That's if "home" was where she actually wanted to be, and this wasn't just another runaway situation. But it seemed unlikely—she was old enough now that she would have soon been making her own way through life. Maybe she was just caught up somewhere—a party, a brothel perhaps? Although, looking around at the stern, armour-plated Iyr, I couldn't imagine that either parties or brothels were in particularly heavy supply around here.

No. If I found her, it would be down to my own abilities as an investigator, rather than dumb luck. Perhaps this was why Saotchun was so keen on using this case as a test.

I looked around at the city I found myself in. The central stronghold, which operated as the capital here on Z'h'ar, was a desolate place—even for a desert planet. High walls surrounded the vertical city, guard towers posted around every gate. In the city itself, everything was about function; there was no art, no music, only blank screens posted on every street corner. This wasn't a planet that I would be returning to for a holiday.

The local Iyr kept to themselves, heads facing down, walking with purpose as though they *all* had somewhere that they desperately wanted to be.

Outside the city, as far as I could tell, was no better. On the plus side, there were none of these charmless Iyr about. On the other hand, they had to deal with a lack of air conditioning, which I didn't myself fancy in this heat.

I thought it was supposed to be winter here? What do they do in their summers? Melt?

The target, Melonaitopila (which was supposedly a *short* name for an Itagurinatipilazutinafi), had, by all accounts, last been spotted at a local U'kka shop. The store, while indeed serving U'kka, seemed to in fact specialise in Guran kebabs—a rather grandiose term for what turned to be simply a rodent cooked on a stick. When it came to my turn to order, I stuck to drinks only.

'Say…,' I started, 'Have you seen this woman, recently, by any chance?'

I showed the store owner a picture of the target on my console's holodisplay. The Iyr shook his head.

'Not seen her.'

'Are you sure?' I prompted. 'She was here, about a week ago?'

'In this store?'

'Yes. In this store.'

'I have not seen her,' the Iyr repeated.

I thanked them for their (lack of) help and sat down to drink my U'kka. When the shift changed, I asked the new Iyr behind the counter the same questions and received the same result.

This wasn't a great start—and it wasn't as though I had a massive number of leads I could follow. I repeated the experiment outside the store, but found that Iyr were unwilling to stop for a stranger from another world. Even when I stood in their way, many would ignore me, and the few who did stop were less than helpful. The local Iyr would have had me believe that nobody had seen this woman.

I'd landed fairly late, so the day soon turned to night. Not wanting to be standing around in a strange street after dark, I decided to abandon my post, regroup, and try again tomorrow. Maybe, if I was lucky, a new route of investigation would occur to me by then.

As I headed in search of somewhere to drink (real drink, not any more U'kka, unless I wanted my bowels to resent me), the screens posted around the city all suddenly blinked into action.

A symbol appeared, glowing in blue on the screens, one that I could have sworn that I recognised from somewhere. An equilateral triangle, with a kind of zig-zag hanging out the bottom. This must have been a character in the Iyr's own language—one that nobody outside their own race was able to understand, even with universal translators. The Iyr really were a private people.

Around me, all the Iyr had stopped to stare at their nearest screen, and were transfixed by it. The symbol was then replaced by an image of an Iyr, sitting, facing the screen. He spoke in the common tongue for a few minutes, during which time, everyone else remained still, silent, fascinated by what they were being told. I listened in; little of it was of interest to me, covering only topics like the local economy, updates on the negotiations with the GMU, and the weather.

Surprise, surprise—it's hot again.

And then, just like that, it ended—the blue shape being shown again, upside down this time, on the screens. The nearby Iyr took this as their cue to continue with their days. I shook my head in bemusement at the whole situation, and I, too, carried on.

I found a bar open just outside the Iyr capital's Central Command building. It was an impressive structure, almost perfectly cubic but for the doors and windows. Stretching across the whole of the front face, two symbols were painted in a brilliantly-white tone, presumably meaning "Central Command" in the local language. I took one last look at this monument to government and then entered the bar.

The Iyr's ambivalence towards the arts meant that their interiors were minimalist, functional. A smooth, concrete bar stood tall along one side of the room, sharp, square corners matching the style of the Central Command building. I assumed this similar motif was unintentional rather than designed—I couldn't yet imagine an Iyr with that much creativity. Next to the bar itself, a number of (largely empty) bar stools hovered, facing away from the square tables behind them. It was at one of these stools which I sat.

With no bar staff currently in sight, I took a moment to look around at the other customers. A group of Iyr sat, having a quiet, civilised conversation at one of the tables. A young Pritan trained his eye on the Lonely Galaxy's guide to Z'h'ar, and accidentally spilt his green drink down his "I heart Z'h'ar" t-shirt. In the corner, another Iyr sat alone, his helmet marked with a red stripe.

I pulled my console from my pocket, with the intention of looking up the meaning of this red stripe, when the bartender suddenly appeared.

'What would you like?'

'You mean, to drink? Or just, like, generally?'

'To drink,' the Iyr replied, and I could only assume that there was a stern expression under that helmet.

What a humourless bunch.

'Whisky,' I replied. I wasn't risking the local stuff, not after that spit-roasted rat I'd seen earlier.

'Terran or Rykan?'

'The real stuff,' I answered. 'Spelled with an H.'

The barman (or barwoman—it was impossible to tell from under these mechsuits) poured a glass, and I timidly took my first sip. Recognising that it really was the good stuff, I downed the rest of the rather small portion.

The Iyr bartender, still standing and looking at me, poured me another, and asked.

'I shall leave the bottle, shall I?'

I shrugged—and the Iyr correctly construed that response as a "yes". I topped up my glass, filling it to the brim, rather than having barely a splash, as suggested by the bartender's serving.

As I sipped quietly, allowing the warm liquid to run down my throat, I pondered everything that had happened over the past few days.

This job, potentially my last, hadn't gotten off to a good start. I had no real leads, a population of locals entirely dedicated to being unhelpful, and the heat was almost unbearable. No wonder this case had been the bottom of the pile, the last to be picked.

Trying to distract myself from the inevitability of me failing to complete this job, I pulled out Leya's journal and skimmed through it again. It was a waste of time; without knowing how she'd encrypted it, I wasn't going to be able to understand it. Looking through it now, it seemed as though there were sections, each cipher using different character sets. It didn't seem like she had encrypted the whole thing at once, but maybe every now and then, whenever she had the chance? I put the journal away again in a huff; I felt destined to fail with that, too.

I spent another hour and a half or so in wistful contemplation; remembering the days of old, and pondering the route I had in front of me.

Only when I realised that my mood was turning sour, did I look around the room once again; it was time for some company. I didn't fancy wasting my time on any more of the humourless locals—neither the quiet group nor the lone customers with the red markings—and so I fixed my eyes on the Pritan.

Soon, he caught me looking at him, and quickly, embarrassed, shifted his gaze to focus back on his book. I could tell, now, that he was staring at the page, reading the same passages over and over, distracted by me gazing at him. It didn't seem like he was going to take the hint that he should come over.

I sighed, collected my glass and the bottle, and walked over to his table. The Pritan continued to pretend that he was transfixed by his book.

If you like that guidebook so much, why don't you just... step outside and actually experience the planet you're reading about.

I resisted the urge to open with this suggestion, and instead sat opposite him, continuing to look over in his direction. I was conscious, already, that the alcohol was starting to go to my head. I wasn't usually like this; it must have been the heat.

'Good book?' I asked.

'Yeah... yeah, it's good,' the Pritan replied, barely glancing up at me.

'Want some of this?' I offered, pointing at the bottle of whisky. 'It's good.'

As if to reinforce the point, I downed another glass.

The Pritan shook his head.

'So, how comes you're here? On holiday?'

Sensing that he wasn't going to be rid of me any time soon, the

Pritan put down his book and diverted his attention to me.

'I'm... I'm, err,' he began, stuttering over his words. 'I'm just travelling the sector. I just finished studying and... and my dad, he said he'd pay for me to see some of the galaxy.'

'Ah, I get it. He thought it'd put some hairs on your chest?'

The Pritan, in addition to looking nervous, now looked confused as well. He glanced down at his own, hairless chest. 'Well... I don't know about *that*. But he thought it would be good for me, if that's what you mean.'

'And you've seen a lot, sitting in bars, reading guidebooks?' I asked, hoping the smile on my face would be enough for the Pritan to understand that I was just poking fun at him.

'I've been out, too!' he replied. 'It's just... Z'h'ar's a bit of a... a cold place, isn't it?'

'Tell me about it. That's the reason I chose *you* to come over and bother, rather than this lot.' I nodded my head in the direction of the group of Iyr, who were currently sitting in silence, sporadically sipping from their glasses.

'Oh. I see,' the Pritan responded, and then, when I didn't carry the conversation any further, asked, 'So... so why are *you* here?'

I looked around the room. Nobody seemed to be listening; the group were talking amongst themselves, the lone Iyr was staring into space.

To hell with it, who's gonna care anyway?

'Here for work. Looking for someone. Diplomat's daughter. From Itagurinatipilaz.'

'Good pronunciation.'

'Thanks.'

'So, she's missing?'

I shrugged. 'Seems that way. Chances are I'm wasting my time looking for her. The people here... haven't exactly been helpful. Don't suppose you've seen her?'

I showed my new friend an image on my console's holodisplay. He shook his head.

'Well,' I replied, 'I guess that was a longshot.'

I raised my glass took another gulp.

The Pritan, loosening up a little now, leaned in close. 'What about that guy? You asked him?' He pointed to the lone drinker in the corner.

'What, I wouldn't ask him cos he looks so scary?'

The Pritan pulled a face which suggested that he thought that was *exactly* the reason that I wouldn't have asked him. 'Tell you what, if you do it, I'll pay for a quarter of that bottle you're drinking.'

'Make it half.'

'No,' he responded.

'OK. A quarter it is.'

How could I refuse such a generous offer?

I stood from the table, set my eyes on the Iyr in the corner, and began walking over to him. Catching myself on the edge of one of the tables, I mumbled, 'Ouch,' which was enough to draw the lone drinker's attention. He stared me down as I approached.

'Hi, how're you?' I asked, slurring my words a little, but surely not enough that anybody would notice.

The Iyr remained silent, still, and stared at me.

'I like your... your red bit... up there,' I continued, pointing at the stripe on the Iyr's helmet.

Still, I got no response. Despite this, I carried on talking.

'So, *anyway*, I was looking for this-'

'Leave,' the Iyr interrupted.

'What? Why?'

'I heard your questions. You ask of things that concern only the council.'

'Concern the...,' I began to ask. 'What you on about?'

'The...,' the lonely Iyr started... and then fell silent. For a few moments there was only the vacant stare of the mechsuit's eyes, the inhabitant apparently taking a moment to think about their response.

'No,' the Iyr started up again. 'Leave. No more questions.'

I turned to look over to my new friend, accidentally stepping on the Iyr's foot in the process. They grunted a noise of irritation, but didn't wince, so I acted as though it hadn't happened.

My friend shrugged—and I shrugged back at him in response. Not wanting to shout across the bar, I mimed in his direction the action of taking a sip of drink. He nodded; he would indeed pay for the promised amount of whisky.

I walked back towards him, meaning to skirt around the quiet group of Iyr, but accidentally collided with one as they stood up. Their drink was knocked from their hand, spilling as the glass dropped to the table, a *clunk* echoing around the bar.

For a moment there was only silence, and then the Iyr whose drink I had spilt raised their arms at me, throwing a punch in my direction. I tried to dodge it, and the blow was softened—as it only barely caught my arm.

So these Iyr aren't so dull after all!

'Bit of an over-reaction, don't you think?' I asked as I stuck my foot forward to sweep my assailant's leg. 'All I did was-'

The Iyr dodged my attempt to floor them. Now even more enraged, they struck me in the side of the head, dizzying me, and sent me tumbling to the ground. They stood over me, broadening their shoulders as though trying to intimidate me.

Through their legs, I saw the Iyr in the corner stand up, and begin marching towards us. When they, too, noticed this, the rest of the Iyr scattered in fear.

'Cease!' the lonely Iyr called out as they strode. 'I will abide no more of this!'

At first, I thought they were directing this at the rowdy group of Iyr—but then I saw that they were staring fixedly at me.

'You *shall not* cast these kinds of aspersions about the Iyr.'

5. Where You Belong

ootsteps pounded the ground around me as the group of four fled the scene. The Iyr who had been drinking in the corner, a red stripe across their helmet, stormed towards me. I didn't need to see this Iyr's face to know that they were furious with me—the body language said it all. And—let's face it—this was a reaction I'd provoked dozens of times before.

As he got closer and closer, I suddenly found myself fearing for what was about to happen. I'd seen, just a few seconds ago, how the Iyr liked to respond to even the most innocent of frustrating situations—and if they were intimidated enough by this one to run away, then it didn't exactly bode well for me.

At the last second, the bartender stepped between us.

'I will handle this, sir,' they told the charging Iyr.

"Sir"? So was that stripe some measure of seniority, perhaps?

The other Iyr slowed to a halt, breathing furiously. They looked at the bartender, then to me, then back to them again. 'If you must,' they replied, before returning to their seat.

My saviour turned to face me.

'Thanks, I guess,' I said to them.

'You are causing a scene. Get out.'

'Oh.'

So much for "my saviour".

I remained still on the floor for a few moments longer.

'Why? All I did was accidentally knock a drink over, surely that happens all the time in here...'

The Iyr shook his head. 'It does. That is not why you need to leave.'

They turned their head to peek over at the Iyr in the corner. He had returned to his drink—but glanced up sporadically.

'If you upset the Head of Guard, then you cause trouble for my business.'

Head of Guard, eh? Very fancy title.

'Upset them? I asked them a few questions, that's all.'

'Yes,' the bartender replied. 'But asking those sorts of questions around here... often means you are never seen again. If my customers start disappearing, the rest will stop coming. You understand?'

'What, I'll be taken away somewhere just for asking where someone is?'

They groaned. So far, the only emotions I'd been able to elicit from the locals had been irritation and rage, which was saying something, even for me. 'Stop asking about it.'

'No!' I retorted, and the volume of my own voice caught me off-guard. Maybe I *had* had a little too much to drink.

'Look,' they continued, leaning in so that they could whisper. 'The last I heard, the woman you are looking for was heading out into the Wastelands. Somewhere near Te'r'ok. Is that enough information to make you leave?'

I nodded.

'Good,' they replied, and then pulled me to my feet by my arm. Raising their voice once again, they called out, 'And do not come back to this establishment! We do not need your sort in here.'

They threw me out onto the street, and, in my drunken state,

I only just about managed to remain on my feet. I looked around. The city was emptier now, only a few stragglers still walking or shuttling about. At this time in the early morning, you might even describe the atmosphere as peaceful. I could take in the sights and enjoy the slightly cooler temperature—as the sun was only just rising against the horizon, hidden still behind the tall stronghold walls. Suddenly the city seemed like an oasis of calm.

I walked south, towards the perimeter gate, hoping to get a view of the wastelands beyond the stronghold's wall. As I approached, the guard towers loomed over me, two monoliths of such great height as would strike fear in the hearts of any invading force. Not that the Arellians, as far as I knew, stood any chance against the Iyr, were they to venture out of their humble lands.

At the base of the towers, there was a transmat station, presumably intended to save the guardsmen from having to climb the hundreds (if not thousands) of steps to the top. There didn't seem to be anyone guarding it, nor were there any signs saying not to use it, so I stepped in for a look at the lands beyond.

The transmat whirred into life and shot me upwards at a rate I'd never experienced before.

Weren't there laws about these kinds of things?

Reaching the top in only a few seconds, I began to feel nauseous—although it was possible that the alcohol was as much to blame as the transmat. I plodded out of the transmat area and held myself against a nearby pillar, counting on it to hold me upright.

A lone guard looked warily on—but said nothing.

When I'd largely recovered from the journey up, I looked out through the glass. As far as the eye could see, desert dunes paved the land of the beyond, looking almost as though they were the waves of the great seas of Terra. But, no, they were still, peaceful, and proudly golden. The sun, rising to the south-east, cast shadows from the great dunes, peppering the land with darker patches, and illuminated small Arellian settlements in the distance. Compared to the stronghold, they seemed like nothing more than villages, like small tribal encampments like in the Terran days of old. Conversely, the few Iyr buildings that stood a few kilometres outside the city limits were tall, piercing the skyline, spoiling an otherwise beautiful view.

I remained up here for a few more minutes, until the glare of the guard became excruciating, and then prepared myself for the transmat back down. It didn't seem so bad on the return journey; I only had to rest for a few seconds at the bottom.

As I rested, I heard a commotion in the distance. Looking down the road, I saw two guards hauling a person along by the arms. I didn't recognise the species; blue, lanky, their hands in weird proportions compared to the width of their limbs. This blue person didn't seem to be resisting in any way, only meekly submitting to being dragged along.

I followed at a distance, this situation having piqued my curiosity. What crime had this person committed to deserve such a treatment?

Probably spilt someone's drink.

When the guards reached the perimeter of the city, they threw the person onto the ground, in much the same way as I had earlier been thrown out by the bartender.

I suspected that I had skimmed over the section of the Z'h'ar guidepage that referred to the Iyr's hobbies:

"The Iyr, a quiet people, typically enjoy throwing people around and just being generally lairy."

'Go. Back to where you belong,' one of the guards muttered at their victim—and then turned to leave them, alone, on the ground.

They were an Arellian, then, this blue creature. The guidepage hadn't had a picture of them; presumably, this wasn't because such an image didn't exist, but because the Arellians were such an unimportant footnote in terms of information about Z'h'ar.

The Arellian stood up—but only once the guards had turned their back on them and left them well alone.

I looked on at the Arellian for a moment, as they stood, motionless, eyes surveying the city in front of them as though they were considering coming back in.

They caught me staring at them and we held eye contact for a few moments, before they turned, shoulders slumped, to trudge back out into the wastelands.

I thought about approaching them, but, what with all the trouble earlier for something as innocent as asking a question, I thought it best to not be seen associating with an apparent criminal. Instead, I walked up to a local salesman, who was pitched up outside the city gates and seemed to be renting shuttle-bikes to clueless tourists.

'How much?' I asked them, knowing better than to try opening with small-talk with an Iyr.

'Three thousand units,' he replied.

'To buy?' That was rather cheap, in fact, I'd thought.

'To rent. One rotation.'

'Oh,' I replied, not bothering to hide the disappointment on my face. 'Bit rich for me, I'm afraid.'

'In that case,' the Iyr went on, 'We shall do a deal. Three thousand units for two rotations.'

'Oh, we're haggling? I can do that! Three thousand units for seven rotations?'

'No. Not seven.'

'For… five rotations?' I asked, hesitantly.

'Three.'

I remained silent for a second, prompting the merchant to continue, 'And I will throw in a free Guran. My partner made too many for me. I am on a diet.'

I shook my head. 'No, thanks, keep the rat. Three thousand units, for three days, and you tell me how to get to Te'r'ok.'

'Deal,' the Iyr replied. 'The easiest way: follow the road to WS1, and then head south-east, not far by bike.'

'WS1?' I asked as I transferred the units to the merchant using my console.

'Outpost. Outpost WS1,' the Iyr explained, and then, only after checking that the units had been transferred, asked, 'Why do you wish to head to Te'r'ok? It is an Arellian village. There are only barbarians out there.'

I shrugged. 'Just trying to see everything while I'm on your lovely planet.'

The Iyr seemed convinced by my answer, even though I'd described Z'h'ar as a "lovely planet", which was obviously a lie. The merchant pulled out a shuttle-bike—a dirtier, older model— and handed it to me.

'Any chance I could get a newer one?' I asked.

'You paid three thousand units. Three thousand gets you this one.'

I shook my head in exasperation, sat on the bike, and started the engine.

Despite being an older model, there was still a huge kick to the acceleration when I pulled on the throttle. If I pulled on it too hard, I feared I would be sent flying off the back. It felt as though these had been designed, really, with only the heavier Iyr in mind, and not *dainty* and *delicate* tourists like myself.

As I shot through the desert, I soon saw a figure in the distance. I slowed as I passed, hoping for a glance at them, and I recognised the figure as the Arellian from earlier—the one who had been in trouble with the Iyr.

My kind of person.

We made eye contact again—only for a split second this time, though, being that I was speeding past him on a shuttle-bike. I wasn't sure I wanted to hang around a so-called "barbarian" anyway.

The road was flat, cutting through the dunes, and took me safely west for a few kilometres. I got a chance to have another look at the outside of the city. It really was built to be imposing, I now realised—a fortress to keep the Arellians at bay.

Soon I came to a junction. A road sign, protected against the sand and dust by a sonar barrier, told me I would need to turn left for Outpost WS1. I did, just this once, as I was told.

The outpost loomed in front of me—one of the few Iyr buildings outside the city limits, which I'd earlier decided ruined the view. If it had been inside the city, it would have seemed like one of the smaller structures, however, out here in the desert, it was still large enough to be striking.

I took a breath in the shadow of the building; the heat, once again, was building and a thudding pain was growing in my head. Terrans really weren't built for this kind of climate. I removed from my satchel my trusty water bottle and took a swig. Over six millennia of Terran civilization, and we still hadn't come up with a better system for hydration than just carrying around water in a bag.

'You can't be here,' I heard a voice call from over my shoulder. An Iyr guardsman leant out of the door to the outpost.

'I'm sorry?'

'You cannot be here. Iyr only.'

'I'm just taking a rest in the shade, that's all.'

'It does not matter. You cannot be here. You are lucky you are not an Arellian, I might have shot you.'

I shook my head. *Alright, misery guts.*

'Move,' the guardsman reiterated, moving his arm to his phaser.

I put my hands in the air. *Don't shoot!*

'Alright, alright. I'm moving, I'm moving,' I told the guard. 'No need to start killing tourists, yeah?'

I packed my water bottle back into my bag, took a breath, and headed back out into the heat, where my shuttle-bike was parked. My break in the shade hadn't been enough; the sun was still bearing down hard, and the pain in my skull kept growing. I started the engine with one last look at the guard, who was still staring on—and zoomed off in a roughly south-easterly direction.

Now off-road, I had to become more confident navigating the dunes. I was hesitant at first, taking them slowly, but as soon as I became sure that the shuttle-bike could hover over the troughs sufficiently, I sped back up. Before long, I was speeding up them, jumping off the peaks, getting some air before the bike had a chance to register the change in height and plummet back down again.

If my head wasn't pounding harder now, with the sun bearing down on it, I would have taken a longer route, enjoyed myself more; but, sadly, that was not to be. I tried to ignore the throbbing pain in my head and continued onwards.

Soon, I saw a small Arellian village in the distance. They really were like the old Terran tribal settlements: small huts, made from more primitive materials, were scattered around what resembled a central socialising area. I pulled at my throttle to get closer for a better look.

As I approached the village, I saw a movement out of the corner of my eye. I slowed, hoping to glimpse it again, but there was nothing. My head was hurting too much to focus on anything while I was moving, so I came to a stop on the side of a dune. I put my hand to my face, trying to shield my eyes from the sun so that I could see better.

A figure was approaching—not fifty metres away. Was that... an Arellian?

The sun was higher in the sky now, and, without the shade and air conditioning units of the stronghold, I was really struggling to ignore the thumping sensation in my head. My body, too, began to feel weak, heavy.

Ack. If I was in the habit of swearing, now might be a good time.

'Fuck,' I tried out, 'That hurts.'

I looked around. The Arellian was gaining on me, getting closer now. However, in the bright sunlight, as well as the reflection from the sand itself, it was almost impossible for me to see.

Why were they walking towards me? What did this wastelander want with me? I need to get going.

I stepped backwards, towards the dune, trying to get to higher ground in case of an attack, but my leg gave way beneath me. I fell to the ground and my vision began to dim.

Laying on the sand, I tried to blink my vision back. My eyes weren't having any of it, though, and, what's more, I started to feel like I was going to throw up.

I felt the sand move around me as the Arellian approached.

It was at this point that I realised just how much trouble I was in. I was weak, collapsed, and the only people who could possibly help were the local barbarian population.

My head was searing with pain now. I could no longer think straight.

I glimpsed the Arellian standing over me, wide blue eyes staring down.

My fate was in their hands.

'Fuck,' I uttered one last time—before I vomited and passed out.

6. Te'rnu

When I awoke, an Arellian was fanning me with a dry, browned leaf. I was in a small hut, lying on a bed, with a good number of other Arellians standing around me, staring in fascination with their wide, blue eyes.

'Give them space,' one of the wastelanders told the others, and all but the one cooling me stepped backwards.

The Arellian who seemed to be in charge looked around at them with exasperated eyes.

'I mean for you to leave,' they reiterated. The group dissipated, leaving me with just the two of these strange folk. As I blinked my vision back into focus, I recognised the Arellian with the leaf as the one who had been escorted out the stronghold earlier in the day.

'I...,' I started to speak, but found my throat dry, little noise escaping from it.

One of the remaining Arellians put a small bowl to my mouth, filled with a red-brown liquid.

'Drink,' they instructed. I sipped at the medicine, taking only a small mouthful at first.

'You were poisoned,' the Arellian told me. They were looking at me with kind eyes, concerned eyes—not the sort of eyes I would have expected to see on a so-called barbarian.

'Was it the Iyr?' the other wastelander asked, wide eyes looking up at me.

'Poisoned?' I asked, voice hoarse. 'No... I wasn't poisoned... I was just... drinking...'

'Drinking?'

'You know... like, alcohol,' I explained.

The two Arellians looked at each other with blank faces. I waved dismissively.

'For fun? Tastes good, takes the edge off?' I added.

They still both looked lost. 'What is "the edge"?'

I shook my head. 'It doesn't matter. It was just the heat getting to me, anyway, I think.'

'You come from a cold place?' asked the one in charge.

'Yeah, I...,' and then I trailed off, instead asking, 'Do you have water?'

The leader nodded, turned to the other Arellian, and said, 'Te'rnu, get this one water. Much of it.'

'Yes, Elder.'

Was that a name or a title?

Te'rnu rushed out, and it was just the two of us now.

'That one saved you, you know. They had been away—who knows where they had gone this time—and found you as they returned to us. Carried you here.'

'Yeah? I'll make sure to say thanks.'

'Do. They need to feel valued, that one.'

Te'rnu came rushed back into the hut, clasping a bowl of water in their hands. I drank at it hungrily, finishing the whole thing before I even stopped for a breath.

They continued to stare, eyes wide.

'What is it? Do I have something on my face, or...?' I asked.

'No,' the Elder replied, 'It is just that we have only once seen a creature like you before. Like you... but different. You are... a spaceman?'

I smiled. 'Yeah. Yeah, I guess I am.'

I'd never been the first Terran someone had seen before.

'What do we call you?' Te'rnu asked.

'You mean... my name, or my species?'

'Both! Everything! Tell us all that is out there!' they answered.

'Hush, Te'rnu,' the other Arellian interrupted. 'Don't bother them. They need rest. There will be time for this later.'

They put a hand on my shoulder, gently instructing me to lean back to the bed again.

'Relax,' the Elder whispered. 'There is no rush.'

I soon fell asleep once again.

⤳

It wasn't until the sun was low in the sky once again that I awoke. Between staying up all night drinking and suffering from heatstroke, maybe my broken sleep schedule shouldn't really have been a surprise.

I sat up, slowly, testing how painful moving was going to be. Short of a headache and some achy muscles, I didn't feel too bad—whatever medicine the Arellians had given me had worked.

In the corner of the room, wide blue eyes stared at me.

'Hello, Te'rnu.'

'Hello. How do you feel? Can I ask you questions? Have y-,' they started, only to be interrupted by the Elder returning to the room.

'I see you are awake. Has Te'rnu been bothering you?' the Elder asked.

'No, not at all, he-,' I caught myself. Was Te'rnu a he? I decided to bite the bullet. 'I'm sorry, is it "he"?'

Te'rnu looked confused, so the Elder stepped in to help him out. 'We do not have such concepts. We all act as one.'

'Oh! Erm, so... in terms of...,' I began to ask, trying to feel out whether this question would be deemed as offensive.

This time, it was Te'rnu who helped me out. '"He" is fine. For me, at least.'

He flashed me a smile.

The Elder continued, 'The others typically use "they", but I would doubt they would care, if I am to be honest with you.'

'What... what would I say if I were to describe you, then?' Te'rnu asked.

'"She",' I told him.

Te'rnu smiled again, the concept amusing to him, and began to try the word out. '*She*. I like that! *She* is here. *She* is good.'

'She is!' I confirmed.

The Elder flashed me a look, and I remembered what she had told me during the brief time that I was conscious earlier in the day—that Te'rnu had been the one to save me.

'Hey, erm, Te'rnu...,' I started, and the Elder slid outside. 'Thanks for saving me earlier. I think there's a lot of people on this planet who wouldn't bother.'

Te'rnu smiled again, brilliantly white teeth catching the glare of the sun. 'That is OK, we all need to look out for each other in this world. You think the Iyr would not have helped you?'

'I suspect not,' I replied.

Te'rnu nodded. 'I think not too. But do not tell the Elders I said this.'

'Elders? There's more than one?'

'Yes! The Elder you have met, Elder Ra'ntu, is a gifted doctor, but there are others too. All the older Arellians in this village are Elders. That is... all except me.'

Te'rnu's furrowed brow gave away how irritated this fact made him—a strangely Terran trait.

'Why's that?' I asked.

'They do not trust me.'

He shook his head—as if ridding himself of these thoughts.

'Can I ask you questions now? I've always wanted to meet a spaceman.'

'Go for it,' I replied, 'Seems like a fair trade for saving my life, after all.'

'How many? How many questions would be a fair trade?'

I smiled; there was an endearing level of innocence about the Arellian sitting in front of me. 'Loads.'

'But how many? I shall have to prioritise.'

'I'll tell you when you're running out.'

This seemed to satisfy Te'rnu as an answer, and he jumped straight into the questions.

'How many planets are there?'

'Oh, err, countless. Hundreds of thousands. Millions, maybe, even.'

Te'rnu's eyes widened like a child seeing a magic trick for the first time.

'Only a small handful actually support life, though.'

'What is your planet called?'

'Terra.'

'Terra? That's a pretty name. And, erm...,' Te'rnu paused, a sudden shyness overcoming him. 'And what is... what is *your* name?'

Whoops. I'd forgotten that bit.

'It's Syl. Syl Raynor. Sorry. I should have told you that already, really. I'm still a bit out of it, I guess.'

'Syl-raynor is a pretty name too,' Te'rnu added, no longer making eye contact.

'Just "Syl" is fine.'

'Syl.'

'Yeah.'

He went quiet for a moment, processing everything that I had been telling him, and then question after question began to escape his lips.

He asked about Terra, about what life had been like there. He asked how we travelled amongst the stars. He asked why I looked different to him, and whether other aliens looked different too. He asked and asked and asked until I was seriously considering telling him there actually *was* a limit to how many questions he was allowed.

Finally, a ringing noise came from outside. Te'rnu's eyes lit up again.

'Dinner! Do you have dinner on Terra?'

'We have dinner, yeah. My favourite part of the day,' I answered.

'Mine too,' Te'rnu replied, grinning. He stepped over to where I was laying, grabbed my hands, and pulled me to my feet.

'Thanks, Te'rnu.'

As he led me towards the door, I glanced back at my bag, which was being left alone, at the side of the bed.

'Oh, Te'rnu, will my bag be OK in there?'

He looked confused. Again. This was becoming a real regular occurrence.

'Yes. Why would it not be?'

'Nobody would steal it?'

Te'rnu didn't reply, only maintaining his perplexed expression. I took this as an answer.

Out in the centre of the village, the inhabiting Arellians were sat in a large circle. All held food bowls in front of them, some full, some about to be filled. Te'rnu handed me an empty bowl, and we sat down at a gap in the circle.

To the side of the circle, I noticed, was a tall antenna—next to some kind of screen. It stuck out like a sore thumb in this Arellian village; they were centuries off this kind of technology. It had to have been placed here by the Iyr.

On the side of the antenna, I noticed, was a big red button. Every fibre of my being immediately wanted to push it—how could someone resist a temptation like that?

I turned my attention away from the Iyr technology and back to my hosts. The Arellian who was serving the food poured it into my bowl with a kind smile on his face.

'This is Elder Or'ane,' Te'rnu told me. 'They are in charge of meals.'

I thanked Or'ane, and then, when they were further away, Te'rnu leaned in close, and whispered, 'That is the role *I* wanted.'

I poked timidly at the food. It was curry-like in texture, viscosity, colour, like the dhal that an old boyfriend of mine used to make. I sipped a mouthful. It didn't taste like dhal, but that didn't mean it was bad. There was a sweetness to it, that Terrans wouldn't normally have in their savoury dishes.

'You like it?' Te'rnu asked, eyes wide with hope.

'I do. It's very sweet. If this is how sweet your main course is, then I can't imagine what your second course will be like.'

'What did you say? *Second* course?' Te'rnu asked.

Whoops.

I shook my head. 'Nothing. Ignore me.'

He happily did, and instead continued to sip away at his bowl. I finished mine, too, and resisted the urge to burp. There was no knowing what was offensive to different cultures, so I tended to play it safe when it came to this sorta thing. Maybe they didn't even know what burping was! I kinda liked the idea of the whole circle seeing me do it and wondering what on Terra that was all about.

No, Syl. Resist. Resist!

'Te'rnu, I... I have to ask.'

63

'What is it?'

'I'm curious, I've never met a species without gender before.'

'You want to know how it works? Biologically?'

'Yeah, like... can you get pregnant?'

'I can.'

'And you can also impregnate people?' I asked, and then, in order to diffuse the awkwardness that maybe only existed in my mind, teased, 'Not that I have anything planned.'

'I can impregnate people too, yes.'

'So is that all in one organ? Or do you have, like two different things, each with their own purpose? And you just choose which one you're going to use? Sorry if this is weird to ask. I'm just interested.'

'Maybe we don't talk about this at dinner,' Te'rnu suggested, and suddenly it seemed like he was the more mature out of the two of us.

I looked around the circle. Most—if not all—of the local Arellians were stealing glances in my direction. When I made eye contact with them, most would look away, embarrassed.

I felt a hand on my shoulder. Looking up, I saw Elder Ra'ntu. 'Please, excuse them,' she told me. 'It is only because they have never seen an off-worlder before.'

I smiled an answer back at her, and she patted me on the shoulder three times, before moving around the circle to find an empty space herself.

I turned to Te'rnu.

'Can I ask, how do you survive out here?'

'What do you mean?' he replied.

'In these plains. There can't be much to live on.'

'There are plenty of plants around, if you know where to look. We farm some, in the shade of a hill, not too far away. We keep what we can, which is usually enough, but of course the Iyr take

64

their share.'

'What-' I began, but suddenly the screen buzzed into life, illuminating the circle with a blue hue.

That same blue symbol appeared again—the one I'd seen before the broadcasts in the city. And, just like last time, everyone around me was transfixed by the message to follow. The only difference in the broadcast out here was that it was in a language that my universal translator could understand.

It spoke of crop harvests declining, of where and how the Arellians might farm more food. The locals nodded along, grateful for this information, some even bowing their heads in respect. Only Te'rnu watched the broadcast with a snarl.

As the announcement ended, I saw the symbol yet another time. This time, however, it clicked where I'd seen it before.

I shot up from my feet, alarming Te'rnu and some of the other Arellians around me. I rushed back into the building where I'd been resting and pulled Leya's journal from my bag. I skimmed through it—until I stopped at the section I was looking for.

Sure enough, there it was: that same symbol.

Leya had been here. On Z'h'ar.

Suddenly I had hope that I would see my sister again.

7. The Arellian Conspiracy

I turned to see Te'rnu standing in the doorway, a curious look upon his face.

'Is everything OK?' he asked.

'Yes, it's just...,' I started, then walked outside again, Te'rnu following. 'What was that? On that screen?'

'Oh. It was the daily broadcast. Updates on-'

'Yeah, but the symbol—what was the symbol?' I asked.

'It is... the Iyr's Central Command. Their...,' he trailed off, trying to find the word. 'What do they call it? Their... government.'

And why might a symbol like that be in Leya's journal?

'They are the ones we have to pay tribute to,' Te'rnu continued. 'The ones for whom we have to farm food, metals, everything.'

'Why? What's in it for you guys?'

Te'rnu shook his head. 'I cannot talk about it. It is a private matter. Only an Arellian would understand. And, besides, I am not even sure that I can answer that question and be sure I am telling you the truth...'

There was a certain solemnity to Te'rnu's expression which

stopped me from pressing the subject any further. Instead, I glanced back down at the encrypted journal in front of me.

'What's it mean? That symbol,' I asked. 'Like, I know what it *signifies*, if its the logo of the Central Command... but what does the symbol *mean*?'

Te'rnu shrugged. 'I do not know. None of us here will know. That is the language of the Iyr. Only *they* will know.'

I pulled out the journal and showed Te'rnu the relevant section. 'All these symbols, on these pages, are they all from that language?'

He nodded.

'How would I go about translating this?' I asked.

Te'rnu looked at me warily. 'Theoretically, any Iyr would be able to do that for you, if it is a simple translation. If it is using their code... you would need to log on to a console that's connected to the Central Command's mainframe.'

'Interesting,' I replied—and then voiced the obvious question. 'How do you know all this, Te'rnu?'

He shrugged. 'I have been investigating for a few years now. Most of my life, really.'

'And how old... *are* you?'

'Twenty. I know; I am old.'

I raised my eyebrows. 'If you're old at twenty, then I'm absolutely ancient. People from Terra are normally not even finished with their studies at this age.'

'Their studies?' Te'rnu asked, brow furrowed.

I took a moment to work out how to explain this one. 'Yeah... like... learning all the things they need to know for their jobs.'

Te'rnu laughed, eyes wide. 'It takes them twenty cycles for this? Farmers: you put seeds in the soil, you add water. Cooks: you put food on a fire. What more is there that they need to know?'

'I...,' I began to reply, then shrugged. 'I guess we've over-complicated it where I'm from.'

My Arellian friend looked at me again. Not that he hadn't been looking at me already, but this time... he was *really* looking, almost as though his eyes were piercing into my soul.

'What did *you* study?' he asked.

I sighed. 'You'll laugh.'

'Why would I laugh?'

'Because it'll seem ridiculous to you.' I wasn't sure I could name a single concept that would be more alien to Te'rnu than the answer to his question.

'I will not laugh.'

'Is that a promise?'

'It is a promise, Syl Raynor,' he replied. The addition of my name to this reply added a level of sincerity that was maybe unwarranted for such a topic of conversation.

'Marketing,' I answered.

'What is that?'

Hmm. Well... at least he wasn't laughing.

'Like... making people buy things.'

'Buy? Like the Iyr do? Getting things in exchange for money?'

'Yeah, exactly. So-'

'The Iyr,' Te'rnu interrupted, 'They are always after money in exchange for information. But I do not have money, where do they think this would be coming from?'

He shook his head to himself.

'So how do you *make* people buy things? At phaserpoint?'

'What? No! Just, like, with adverts,' I answered, and then—when Te'rnu's confused face made me realise my mistake—I explained, 'Adverts are images that tell you about products. Or services.'

I breathed deeply, buying myself a short period of time in which to collect my thoughts.

'And I used to work out where the best places to display these adverts were. That whole thing used to be a lot harder, and then we left the GMU—which was significant because it meant our laws changed. Suddenly we could start using data collected by console to target our ads.'

I noticed that Te'rnu's eyes had glazed over.

'So... if I was on Terra and was talking with someone about how I didn't like how I had got this new mole on my trip to Turknan, 'cos the sun there is so strong, then I might start seeing ads for UV protection injections, or replacement skin grafts. You see?'

Te'rnu paused for a moment. 'And why did you cease doing this?'

I shrugged. 'When Leya disappeared it stopped seeming important. I guess maybe I knew it wasn't important all along, but while it was paying the bills... I didn't mind the harm it was doing. But then, when I lost someone... I dunno, I guess it seemed like the galaxy had enough people making people buy things they don't need and not enough people helping people find the things they *do* need.'

There was another moment of silence. It felt as though Te'rnu considered himself out of his depth. Soon his mouth opened once again.

'If you stopped studying a few years ago, then how old *does* that make you?'

'I mean... it's rude to ask a woman her age, and all, but... I'm twenty-four.'

'Twenty-four?!' he repeated, absolutely astounded by this concept. 'You Terrans can live that long?'

'We live up to around, like, a hundred and ten, Te'rnu.'

'A hundred and-,' he started replying, mouth agape. 'Maybe Ur'tna was on to something...'

Before I could get a chance to ask him what on Terra that

meant, there was a scream from one of the buildings.

Te'rnu's head spun to face the source of the noise, and his face turned glum.

He looked at me, pain in his eyes, and said, 'You wanted to know why we pay tribute to the Iyr? It looks like you are about to find out.'

A crowd was quickly amassing about the entrance to one of the huts, everyone in it wearing a frown upon their faces. From inside, the groans and screaming continued. It sounded as though someone was being tortured in there.

Elder Ra'ntu arrived in the doorway, having presumably been checking on the screaming Arellian, and gave a nod. Upon receiving this signal, a member of the crowd rushed to the Iyr antenna, and pushed the red button.

The system produced a few beeps, and soon, a countdown appeared on the screen.

'What's that mean?' I whispered to Te'rnu.

'That is how long until they get here,' he replied.

'Who?' I asked.

'I think you know the answer to that question,' replied Te'rnu. He was right; I most certainly did.

⇥

Sure enough, the Iyr soon arrived. A small shuttle floated down from the sky, landing just outside of town. The exhaust from the vehicle scattered the remaining bowls and food from dinner, but none of the Arellians seemed to care about that at this moment.

Two Iyr jumped off the back of the ship as it landed and strode towards the group of Arellians. One of them noticed me, a Terran, standing among them, and turned their head to stare at me as they walked—but said nothing.

The crowd parted for these two Iyr, allowing them access to

the house, and even Elder Ra'ntu stood aside.

The Arellians clustered back together, blocking my view, so I stepped onto a rock for a better look at what was going on. Inside, the two Iyr crouched down beside the screaming Arellian. They looked at one another, nodded, and then picked the local up by the arms, dragging them back outside and towards the ship.

The other locals, as the screaming Arellian was dragged through them, came together in a hum. It was an almost religious response to the situation, as though it was a ceremony.

'What's happened to them?' I asked Te'rnu.

'They are twenty-one,' he replied. 'They are dying.'

Suddenly I understood why the Arellians were almost childlike in innocence. Even at their oldest, they were barely out of their teens. They didn't even have the chance to develop cynicism, or bitterness, or anything of the like. They were a pure species, and their limited lifespan was the very reason why.

The Iyr loaded the dying Arellian onto the ship—and the engines whirred into life once again. As it took off, the remaining villagers watched him go.

'So... that's it? You never see them again?' I asked. 'No... no more ceremony than that?'

Elder Ra'ntu appeared at our side, and with a hand held to their heart, spoke. 'Once it begins, there is no time for any formalities. They must go.'

'Once what begins?' I asked.

'The Mutation,' Te'rnu replied.

That doesn't sound particularly promising.

Elder Ra'ntu explained, 'As an Arellian grows older, their chances of beginning the Mutation get greater. It happens to all of us.'

'And what exactly *is* this Mutation?'

'The Arellian's loins begin to change. They swell, and they

71

clench. It causes them huge pain.'

'Hence the screaming,' I added.

'Yes. They say that only the Iyr ever experience that amount of pain. Only they can understand what we Arellians go through. That's why we send our mutated to them; they relieve the pain for the dying Arellian as best they can. As soon as the process begins, we summon them, and pray that they do not take long to arrive— for the dying's sake.'

'*That* is why we send tribute,' Te'rnu added. 'Supposedly.'

Elder Ra'ntu ignored this last word uttered by Te'rnu. 'They are our saviours. *Some* would do well to remember that.'

Te'rnu, incensed, continued, 'How do we know this? How do we know they are doing anything at all to help our dead? We have no evidence!'

'No, Te'rnu,' Elder Ra'ntu replied, raising their voice for the first time in my presence. 'We have faith!'

'Faith?' Te'rnu replied, outraged by the idea. 'Having faith only means that we know nothing for sure! They are exploiting us, do you not see?'

'I-,' I began, only to get cut off by Elder Ra'ntu.

'Generations upon generations of Arellians have paid tribute in this way. It is not for you to decide to break with tradition! This is *exactly* why you were never made Elder, Te'rnu. And at this rate, you never-'

'What about Ur'tna?' Te'rnu suddenly interjected.

Elder Ra'ntu looked exasperated. 'Do not fill the spaceman's mind with stories of Ur'tna's nonsense. We have already had that Trial, we have already ruled that these stories were little more than the ramblings of a lunatic.'

'Forget the trial! We did not know-'

'Te'rnu!' Ra'ntu insisted. 'Enough! The off-worlder does not need to hear this!'

'I'm happy to hear what he has to say,' I butted in, shooting Te'rnu a smile. 'He saved my life, after all. Who was Ur'tna?' Part of me was just happy to finally get a word in.

Te'rnu shot me a brief smile in thanks. Ra'ntu, on the other hand, looked less than impressed.

'They were an Arellian. Lived here, in Te'r'ok. Ur'tna was absolutely convinced that there was more going on with the tributes than met the eye.'

'And was also... mad,' Ra'ntu added.

'That does not necessarily mean Ur'tna was wrong,' Te'rnu replied.

'That's true! I've known plenty of completely mad people who were almost always right,' I added, trying my darndest to support the person who'd saved my life. I was, however, complete ignored by both of them. Old quarrels die hard—on Z'h'ar as it was in Terra.

'Nobody else ever believed Ur'tnu,' Te'rnu continued, 'But Ur'tnu was convinced that the Iyr were doing something with the people they had taken.'

'Like what?' I asked.

'Experimenting on them? Enslaving them? Selling them? Ur'tnu never quite got to the bottom of it.'

'All little more than conspiracy theories!' Ra'ntu interjected. 'Please don't pay attention to this one, spaceman. Te'rnu's mind was warped by Ur'tnu's babbling, and it never quite recovered, it seemed.'

I was already fascinated by the idea of there being a conspiracy, though. Who more likely than the irritable, foul-tempered Iyr to be behind some sort of scheme like this?

'Did Ur'tnu ever get any proof?' I asked.

'Not really,' Te'rnu answered. 'But there was this one thing. Towards the end, they kept repeating this one idea: that the

Mutation doesn't have to be the end for us. That we can live through it, but the Iyr do not want us to. Maybe we get too powerful, or smart, or some other trait which might give us more of an advantage than the Iyr want us to have. It was not until Ur'tnu said *this* that they disappeared.'

'Ignore this one, spaceman. Te'rnu is at the end of their life. They fear their own mortality, and so they speak these conspiracy theories as a way of avoiding facing that fear.'

'I fear nothing!' Te'rnu argued. 'Well... I fear some things, yes. But not this!'

'And yet you have no proof. Once again, you simply exist to cast doubt upon the Tradition. Tradition which has served this community well, I might add!'

'I have proof!' he shouted. 'That is where I have been! I have found someone inside the Stronghold who was willing to talk with me.'

'You have been *where*?' Ra'ntu asked.

'They told me, Syl, they told me: Ur'tnu didn't just disappear, they were taken.'

'As is the Tradition!' Ra'ntu insisted.

'No! You do not understand! Ur'tnu was taken before the Mutation started. The Iyr, they weren't trying to *save* them, they were trying to *silence* them!'

8. The Face of the Iyr

We spoke long into the night. While Te'rnu, a group of other Arellians, and I sat around the remnants of a once-scorching fire, I told stories of my life so far. I spoke about my childhood, about going to school, about breakups and heartbreak; even the most tedious of stories they were fascinated by. I'd never before had such a captivated audience, and I lost myself in the storytelling.

Once the fire had gone out, and the sky was dark with the dead of night, did I remember why I was out here in the Wastelands.

'Do you guys mind if I ask *you* a question? It has to do with why I'm here.'

They all nodded—almost in unison.

'I'm actually looking for someone. An off-worlder, like me. That's why I'm on Z'h'ar—or, more specifically, here in Te'r'ok. They were an Itagurinatipilazutinafi, although, I guess... you don't know what that is.'

They were now shaking their heads.

'No,' Te'rnu replied, 'Although I suspect we can guess.'

'What's that mean?' I asked.

'There was another, before you, who came here. Looked different to you. They had clearer skin.'

'Well, thanks,' I replied, although Te'rnu didn't seem to recognise the sarcastic undertones.

'They were not here long; we were not able to get much information out of them. Not like *you*.'

'If I show you a picture, can you tell me if it was her?'

Back to the nodding again.

I pulled up my left sleeve, revealing my console. All eyes were trained upon this strange device. I tapped in the relevant commands and brought up the Z'h'ar case file. I put the target's image on the holodisplay.

'Her name's Melonaitopila. She-'

But I stopped when I looked around at the crowd. The wide eyes and continued nodding suggested that this was indeed the person who had been here.

Use your words!

'She was here?' I asked, beginning to wonder if the Arellians treated nodding and shaking their heads to mean different things.

'They were,' one of the Arellians piped up. 'Their hair, though, was different. Not so... pristine, as it is there.'

'And their eyes,' another added.

'What about her eyes?' I prompted.

'There was pain in them.'

Right. Pain. In her eyes. Not exactly much to go on, as far as my investigation was concerned.

'She was scared,' Te'rnu explained.

'Do you know where she went? After she left here?'

The was a moment where I felt the whole group draw a sharp intake of breath. Only Te'rnu seemed to feel comfortable replying.

'She didn't leave. Or, at least, she did not intend to. She was taken.'

'Taken?'

'Just like Ur'ntu was.'

'Why? Did she know something?'

This wasn't a simple run-away case, then, nor just a young woman out doing some partying. This woman really was in trouble. This meant, sadly, that I needed to take this job a whole load more seriously.

There was a longer pause this time, even Te'rnu initially being loath to answer.

'She...,' Te'rnu began, 'She said she saw the face of an Iyr.'

I had a sense that if the Arellians didn't possess such a naturally blue skin tone, they would have gone white at this point. Fear was plastered all over their faces.

'Why is that such a big deal?' I asked. 'I know they're quite shy about it, but...'

'No, you don't understand,' Te'rnu told me. 'Nobody outside of their own race has *ever* seen the Iyr's true face.'

'Well, what did she see?' I asked. 'That got her so scared?'

Te'rnu shook his head. 'We do not know. She was too afraid to talk about it.'

'They were afraid, yes,' a younger Arellian interrupted, 'But they didn't say that was the reason they didn't tell us. They said they didn't think we would *want* to know.'

'*I* wanted to,' Te'rnu insisted.

'But she didn't tell you?' I asked.

'No,' he replied.

'They said it was in our best interest,' the young Arellian confirmed.

'What could she have seen, Te'rnu? You must have some idea. Maybe Ur'tnu said something?'

'The Elders say we shouldn't speak of Ur'tnu,' the youth continued.

'Well, don't tell them, then, Pr'atu,' Te'rnu responded, like a teenager dealing with a nagging younger sibling.

Pr'atu took Te'rnu's point—and went quiet.

'Ur'tnu didn't say anything about this, no,' Te'rnu continued, 'But that doesn't mean to say it's not related.'

I said nothing for a moment, instead trying to work out our next move.

'If I didn't think it could cost me my life, or at least my freedom, I'd say my best chance of finding Melonaitopila would be to get a look at an Iyr for myself.'

The group remained silent, but I could see a sparkle of excitement in Te'rnu's eyes.

⇥

I soon fell back into the rhythm of being interrogated by the Arellians about my past life. It was less passionate, now, with the locals starting to tire, and before long it was just Te'rnu and me by the pile of ash that had, a few hours earlier, been a fire.

Te'rnu had become tense, and I could tell there was something he was hoping to ask me.

'What is it, mate?' I asked.

Now that he felt he had permission to say it, Te'rnu blurted, 'Should you ever see the skin of an Iyr, would you come back, here, and tell me? I would like to know... before I die.'

Cautiously, I nodded. 'OK, Te'rnu. I can do that. But...'

I was feeling like misbehaving; it had been almost a day since I had done anything wicked.

'We could always go take a look for ourselves, now, if you're up for a little spot of mischief?'

Te'rnu looked at me with those wide, wary eyes. '...How would we do that?'

'Is there anywhere we might get an Iyr alone? Force 'em to give us a look?' I asked, a plan already forming in my mind.

The Arellian thought about it, and then, nodding, said, 'Yes. The outpost. There should only be one Iyr at night. Around now.'

'They're not exactly too worried about their security, are they?' I asked.

Te'rnu shook his head. 'Why would they be? They have beaten us into submission.'

'You're up for a little act of revolution, then?' I asked.

He looked at his feet. 'I do not know if I should. If we got caught...'

I clapped my hand to his shoulder. 'Come on, I thought you were Te'rnu—the only Arellian who breaks the rules! The only one too rebellious to be made an Elder!'

'There is a limit, though. Sneaking into the stronghold is one thing, but... assaulting an Iyr? I don't know if they would let me go if I did that.'

'Then let's not get caught!' I replied.

He remained silent, still not convinced by my argument.

I continued. 'Come on, we have a chance to change things for your people here. We can finish what Ur'ntu started. Maybe, then, you guys can have a better life here.'

Te'rnu thought about it some more, and then, nodding to himself ferociously as though psyching himself up, said, 'OK. I will do it—on one condition. They will shoot me on site if I get too close to the outpost, so we must have a plan to stop that from happening.'

'That's not true, I went up there earlier. Took a rest in the shade of the building, and they didn't shoot me.'

'You are not an Arellian, though,' Te'rnu responded.

'I see,' I replied, 'Well, then, let's use that to our advantage.'

There was a scuffling sound behind us. Te'rnu and I both spun our heads around to look for the source. Part of me imagined that it was an Iyr, here, somehow foiling our plan before it ever really began.

But, no, it wasn't them. It was the young Arellian, Pr'atu, who had been outspoken about not repeating Ur'tnu's conspiracies, earlier.

'Pr'atu, what are you doing?' Te'rnu asked.

'How long you been there, buddy?' I added. I didn't trust the young'un to keep this plan to themselves, and I sensed that we wouldn't want the Elders to hear about it.

'Oh, erm…,' Pr'atu responded, 'A little while… You are planning to look upon the Iyr's flesh?'

Te'rnu and I looked at one another.

'I mean, I wouldn't describe it as "looking upon their flesh" because that's a super creepy way to talk about it, but that's the crux of it, yeah. You can keep this to yourself, though, can't you, Pr'atu?'

'I… erm… can I come with you?' the youth replied.

'Why would you want to do that?' I asked.

'I thought you didn't believe in Ur'tnu's theories,' Te'rnu added.

'It is not that I do not believe,' Pr'atu replied, 'Only that I do not want you getting in any more trouble with the Elders for talking about it. So… I can come?'

I looked to Te'rnu for an answer.

'I guess the truth is important for you, too,' he decided.

The three of us soon crept off into the night, heading northeast for Outpost WS1, and leaving the village sleeping behind us.

In the darkness, the outpost used huge lighting units to illuminate the area around it—to a good 150 metres radius. Te'rnu had been right; there was no way we wouldn't be spotted when we approached.

Crouching behind the peak of a dune, just outside of the illuminated area, I turned to Te'rnu.

'Definitely clear on the plan?' I asked.

'You wait for us to get into position, distract the guard, and then we creep up behind them. Then, we remove their helmet. That is it.'

'Yes,' I replied, 'I guess it's not really that complicated a plan, is it. You definitely want to go ahead with this? Last chance to back out.'

Te'rnu nodded. Pr'atu, watching for Te'rnu's response, then nodded as well.

'OK,' I said. 'And if there's more than one guard?'

'There will not be. There never is,' Te'rnu replied.

'OK, yes, but if there is? What's the plan?'

'I guess... we run?' Pr'atu answered.

I shrugged. 'Good enough for me.'

Te'rnu and Pr'atu, keeping low, began to skirt the edge of the outpost's lit radius, and I began to count.

When the predetermined one hundred and eighty seconds had passed, I stood up, and the plan began in earnest.

I walked, as casually as I could manage, straight for the outpost.

As I got closer, I kept expecting to be seen, to be shouted at... but there was nothing.

Was the guard asleep at their post?

I arrived at the door, and, feeling in a particularly risky mood, opened it.

The room inside made up the whole of the ground floor, with the exception of a small transmat room right in the middle. The door to this room was closed, which presumably meant that the guard was asleep up above.

On my left, I noticed something: a computer terminal with

that same symbol on—the symbol of Central Command. This was my chance, I realised, to decrypt some of Leya's journal.

Forgetting, for a moment, about my mission and the two Arellians slowly creeping up on the other side of the outpost, I instead plugged the diary into the computer terminal.

It took me a few moments to muddle through the interface, being that it was in the Iyr's private language. Fortunately, I was familiar enough with dodgy user interfaces to figure it out—I did work on Station 34-Alpha, after all, where the main terminals were nothing if not a complete mess.

A progress bar appeared; this encryption was complicated enough that the local processing power of the machine was struggling to handle it. While it was slow, it was still, just about, working.

That is—until the console started to overheat. What with this planet's high average temperature, this couldn't have been a rare occurrence—and indeed the alert that suddenly popped up confirmed this.

A siren sounded throughout the outpost, designed to alert the inhabitants to the computer malfunction. Instead, however, this seemed to stir the Iyr guardsman into life, who appeared at the exit of the transmat room just as the two Arellians arrived at the main doorway.

'Who are you?' the guard shouted, emerging from the room armed with a huge phase rifle. 'Identify!'

Definitely making up for something, these Iyr are.

Before either Te'rnu or I could think, the young Arellian Pr'atu charged at the Iyr, jumping onto their back and catching them by surprise.

The Iyr, out of reflex, fired a shot from the rifle, hitting and completely frying the computer console that the diary was tapped into.

My heart lurched, just for a moment, before I recognised that the diary was unhurt. I grabbed the journal and ran for cover, dodging the beams as the Iyr fired clumsily around me, the Arellian youth still clinging to his back.

I slid behind a low table, and peered around at Pr'atu and the Iyr. Pr'atu was pulling, now, at the Iyr's helmet, and I could see a glimpse of dark blue skin in the crack that formed.

Te'rnu, having previously been frozen out of fear in the doorway, suddenly realised that Pr'atu needed help, and started rushing towards the tussling pair.

The Iyr stopped firing at me and instead began to focus on the Arellian that was trying to remove their helmet. They jumped backwards, landing on and crushing Pr'atu—and the Arellian's grip was loosened enough that the Iyr wriggled free.

The guardsman pointed their rifle at the young Arellian on the floor, and shouted, 'Stop!' to Te'rnu and I.

Te'rnu ceased moving mid-step.

The four of us remained still, quiet, and each tried to figure out our next move.

It was a stand-off. I could see the Iyr's itchy trigger finger. If either Te'rnu or I approached to save Pr'atu, then we—or Pr'atu—would be fired upon. Pr'atu remained motionless on the floor, also terrified about what might happen if they moved.

Te'rnu and I made eye contact. I tried to communicate "don't move!' to him non-verbally, which was received with only a slightly confused expression.

And then, whether intentionally or not, Te'rnu moved, putting his until-now hovering foot back down on the ground.

That was all the provocation that the Iyr needed. They spun on the spot, pointing the phase rifle at Te'rnu, and began to fire.

Te'rnu dived out of the way, the shot hitting the wall behind him. As another shot charged up, he ran for the door.

83

I edged forwards towards Pr'atu, hoping that Te'rnu would divert the Iyr's attention away for long enough—but I was out of luck on that front too.

Te'rnu leapt out the door, a beam barely missing him as he did so.

Once the older of the two Arellians was out of sight, the Iyr turned to face Pr'atu and me.

I was still over ten metres away from Pr'atu, with no chance of grabbing them before the Iyr could fire.

And then, the guardsman spoke.

'Leave,' the Iyr told me. 'Involving a Terran would reflect badly on me, especially at this critical juncture.'

'Can I take them?' I asked, pointing at Pr'atu.

The Iyr shook their head. 'No. Only you. This one stays.'

'I can't leave without them,' I told the Iyr.

'Then I am forced to take you in.'

The Iyr raised their phase rifle to point at me.

'OK!' I answered, realising that at this point, there was no reason for both of us to be caught. 'I'm sorry, Pr'atu,' I told the young Arellian—and then turned to leave the outpost.

Outside, Te'rnu was waiting.

'What happened back then? Where was the Iyr? Why did you not stick to the plan?'

Te'rnu's eyes were narrowed, angry.

He was perfectly right to be annoyed; this was—at least in part—my fault. If I hadn't been distracted by the terminal, if I had just called for the guard's attention from the doorway, maybe I could have lured him into a better position for the ambush.

But why did Pr'atu have to run at the Iyr like that? Couldn't they have seen that this mission had been a bust?

'We'll get Pr'atu back, Te'rnu,' I told him. 'We're not leaving until we do.'

9. An Investigation On Trial

We couldn't wait long. At any moment, Iyr reinforcements could turn up to take poor Pr'atu away. In fact, if their response time was anything like it had been for the screaming Arellian earlier, then we only had a maximum of around three minutes.

'What are we going to do?' Te'rnu repeated for what must have been the fifth or sixth time.

'I've got... some idea,' I replied.

I fumbled at the device on my right sleeve; this was my only real advantage against an armed guardsman—and I intended to use it.

Te'rnu spotted me touching at my sleeve.

'What is it?' he asked.

'An EMP. Electro-Magnetic Pulse. Disables all electronics in the area. Comes in handy every now and then.'

'Would carrying a phaser not be easier?'

'I don't like phasers,' I snapped at him, and then, when I realised I had sounded vicious, added, 'Sorry.'

Te'rnu ignored the nasty tone— or perhaps was simply

oblivious to it. 'How is this EMP going to help us? It will shut down the lights?'

'Yes. And the phaser too, hopefully.'

'Hopefully?'

'There's a chance the phaser is fitted with a backup battery. If that's the case...'

I trailed off. Judging by the look on his face, Te'rnu seemed to have no trouble filling in the blanks.

'What are the chances of that?'

'I don't know... maybe... ten percent?'

'So one in every ten times that you run into a room like this, you get shot?'

I grimaced in response. 'It usually works out OK.'

Te'rnu and I looked back at the outpost.

'Well... no time like the present, I guess,' I sighed, resigning myself to what I was about to do. I looked over my shoulder at Te'rnu as I began to hurry back to the outpost.

'Stay here.'

I hoped that the lone guardsman was still otherwise preoccupied with their prisoner. If not, then in all likelihood I was about to get shot at.

Hooray.

I prepared myself to jump out of the way.

Luck seemed to be working in my favour; I reached the outside wall without any trouble. Perhaps the Iyr thought they had sufficiently scared us off, and that we wouldn't be coming back any time soon. Perhaps if I had been entirely sane, then the guardsman would have been completely right.

I placed my hand on my right wrist in readiness to activate the EMP—and stepped through the door.

Inside, Pr'atu was pressed up against the transmat room's wall, too afraid to make a break for it and risk being killed. We made eye contact. As soon as the Arellian saw me, they relaxed slightly.

The Iyr guardsman was still in the room, tapping at a computer terminal, their phase rifle rested on the top.

I edged forwards, hoping to only use the EMP at the last possible moment, so I could make the most of the confusion that would inevitably follow.

Suddenly the Iyr stopped typing.

I froze.

They looked up—straight at me.

'Hi again!' I greeted them.

Within the next two seconds, three significant things happened.

First, Pr'atu began to make a sprint for the opposite door, which meant that the Iyr's targets were split—one to their left, one to their right.

Second, the Iyr reached for their rifle, picked it up, and swung it around to point in the direction of Pr'atu. They fired their first beam prematurely, missing the Arellian but instead hitting the controls to the door panel, completely frying them—and making the door itself unusable.

Lastly, I activated the EMP.

With a quiet, deep *whoomph*, the power of the outpost went offline, leaving the room in almost total darkness.

The Iyr, surprised, made some sort of "*acckk!*" noise in exasperation, and instead tried to turn to train their rifle on me. They struggled to move, their mechsuit having jammed up due to the EMP.

Instinctively, I jumped out of the way—but no shot came. All I heard was the familiar clicking sound of an offline phaser failing to discharge.

Now knowing that I was safe, I charged at the Iyr, tacking them to the ground. I flicked my left wrist, releasing my blade, and pressed it on their throat.

'How long do we have? Until more of you get here?'

The Iyr, seemingly unphased, replied, 'At most, two minutes.'

I looked up at Pr'atu. The youth's eyes were wide with terror.

'We should go.'

I nodded—and the Arellian began to run. I gave Pr'atu a few seconds headstart before I, too, began to sprint away from the outpost, releasing the Iyr in the process.

We exited the outpost, still sprinting, and Te'rnu's face dropped when he saw the speed we were travelling at. Without stopping to ask questions, he began to sprint too—back in the direction of Te'r'ok.

Soon an alarm began to blare behind us; the mechsuit hadn't frozen for long, it seemed.

We ran as fast as we could—over the steep dunes, fighting against the loose sand. A few minutes later, I turned back to look at the outpost in the distance.

A shuttle, only now, was landing. They were late.

I called to Te'rnu, drawing his attention to the landed ship.

'Here!' Te'rnu called, pointing at a small outcrop of rock. The three of us jumped in, huddled up tight, and stayed as still as we could, hoping to avoid being spotted.

But more and more minutes passed, and there was no sign that we were being pursued.

Perhaps the Iyr didn't think it was worth the effort, or perhaps they knew better than to try and find Arellians hiding in their own territory. Whatever the reason, we were safe.

Confident now that we'd got away with it, we continued back to town at a slower pace, allowing our aching muscles some respite. As Te'rok came into view in the distance, the sun was beginning to rise, and the other villagers were up and about.

This meant, of course, that they had noticed our disappearance.

'Where have you been?' an angry Arellian called out at Pr'atu. They stormed over to the young one and grabbed them by the arm. 'You do *not* disappear like that, you understand me?'

As they dragged Pr'atu back into the village, they turned to look at Te'rnu.

'And *you*. You should know better.'

Ra'ntu, too, stared at us with an irritated expression upon their face.

'We were just trying to see if we could see an Iyr's face!' Pr'atu argued with their parent. 'Te'rnu says we should know these things!'

Elder Ra'ntu began to speak. 'You drag Pr'atu into this mess? At that age?'

Te'rnu looked down at the floor, ashamed.

'Where did you go?' Ra'ntu asked.

'The Outpost. WS1.'

There was a moment of silence.

Elder Ra'ntu raised her voice when they spoke next—not out of anger, but out of proclamation.

'Te'rnu has exceeded even his own prior recklessness. Te'rnu has brought shame to our village! Te'rnu must be put to trial!'

Ra'ntu paused—and I couldn't help but think that this was only for effect.

'No,' they continued, staring deep into my eyes, 'They *all* must be put to trial.'

I looked to Te'rnu, who stood, despondent, eyes fixed on the ground.

Ra'ntu walked closer to us and whispered so that nobody else would hear, 'Let this be a lesson to you. Nobody breaks with the Tradition.'

⤵

We were ushered into the same building that I'd first been brought to, while the Elders prepared for the trial. Te'rnu and Pr'atu waited anxiously, while I seriously debated simply standing up and leaving.

I couldn't justify leaving Te'rnu, though—not after he'd saved my life. So I stayed—and hoped I could save him from whatever hardship Ra'ntu had planned.

Soon, we were moved into the largest of the village's buildings, which had enough space for about a dozen people.

Three Elders—Ra'ntu, Or'ane, and another that I didn't recognise—sat at the end of the room, on higher chairs, facing the rest of us. No matter where you go in the galaxy, nobody could resist the idea of nothing being higher than justice. It was the *definition* of justice, on the other hand, which seemed to change from planet to planet.

Te'rnu, Pr'atu, and I were sat at the front, on a long, uncomfortable, bench. I looked at the others; what a bunch we were. Like some heroes of old: The Three Musketeers, or the Three Amigos, or the Three... I dunno, Tenors?

No.

In the eyes of everyone around us, we weren't heroes, we were villains. Criminals, even.

Ra'ntu made a noise to draw my attention, and I span back around to face the front.

'We are gathered here to rule on the punishments for Te'rnu, Pr'atu, and the off-worlder, for breaking with the sacred Traditions, and assaulting an Iyr.'

There was a slight whispering behind me, from the trial's onlookers.

'Wait,' I asked. 'So this isn't even about whether we're innocent or not? Just what the punishment is going to be?'

Te'rnu glared at me; obviously speaking at this point was a massive faux-pas in the eyes of the Arellians.

Elder Ra'ntu humoured me. 'The Elders have already convened and determined that the three of you are indeed guilty. I stress, also, that now is *not* the time for you to speak.'

I pulled a face... but said nothing.

'We will first hear from Pr'atu. If you will please stand.'

The youth to my left did as was commanded. I could see them shaking, having succumbed to their nerves. On the opposite side of Pr'atu sat Te'rnu, and I could see that he had recognised the young one's fear too.

'Would you please describe the events that led to you travelling to outpost WS1?' Ra'ntu asked.

Pr'atu took a moment before they responded, the nerves meaning that they were struggling to get words out.

'I, err...,' Pr'atu started, casting a look at Te'rnu and me. 'I was still awake, late, last night, listening to the off-worlder's tales. After a while, they thought-'

'Who is "they", Pr'atu, if you wouldn't mind clarifying?' asked Or'ane, a kind smile on their face.

'Te'rnu and the spaceman,' Pr'atu clarified.

'Thank you. Go on.'

'So they—Te'rnu and Syl—thought everyone else had gone to sleep, and they were discussing the skin of the Iyr.'

Pr'atu paused for questions, but none came.

'And they started talking about how they might see it for themselves. They planned to go to the outpost, and sneak up on the guard.'

'And how did you become involved in this scheme, Pr'atu?'

'Oh. I asked if I could come,' Pr'atu replied.

The Elder gave each other knowing looks—and damning ones, at that.

Uh-oh.

'You are saying that you willingly volunteered to help Te'rnu and the off-worlder break with Tradition?'

'I, err...' Pr'atu looked over at Te'rnu and I for help. We weren't able to give any. 'Yes. I did.'

'Thank you, Pr'atu, I think we have heard enough,' Ra'ntu announced. 'If, Te'rnu, you will please now stand.'

Te'rnu did as he was told, before beginning to talk, unprompted. Even *I* knew that by now, this wasn't right and proper decorum.

'May I speak freely? Before the questions begin,' Te'rnu said, and then continued without waiting for a response. 'It is very kind of Pr'atu to cover for me, but I am afraid their story was not reflective of the truth. It was me, in fact, who convinced Pr'atu to join us.'

'And why would you do that?'

There was a brief pause before Te'rnu replied. Only Pr'atu and I could know that this was because he was inventing a new version of the story.

'Because we needed a third. We though Pr'atu was young, and impressionable—so we encouraged them to join us.'

The Elders remained silent for a few moments, and then Ra'ntu turned to focus on me.

'Is that correct, off-worlder?'

I stood up to address the council. 'Yep! That's right! We convinced Pr'atu to join us. They were resistant at first, but we told them that it was important for the village that they come too.'

I hoped my lying was up to snuff; I could feel the words coming out of my mouth become stilted, unnatural. Elder Ra'ntu nodded in response to this testimony.

'We have one more question for you. Did you hurt the Iyr? Or cause harm to them in any other way?'

Te'rnu shook his head.

'No,' I lied, remembering the damage that we had caused to the outpost and the computer system. 'None at all.'

'Can you confirm this for us, please, Te'rnu.'

He looked at me for a moment, pain in his eyes, and then turned back to the Elders.

'That is correct. No harm was done.'

'Thank you,' Ra'ntu replied. 'I think you three have answered every question we have. We will return momentarily to rule on your punishments.'

The three Elders left the building, and Te'rnu and I sat back down.

'What sort of punishments are normally given out in these?' I asked.

Te'rnu took a moment to respond.

'These are rare, so my experience with punishments are few. Some are assigned work to do, to benefit the community, and others...'

Te'rnu paused.

'Others... what?' I prompted, dreading the answer.

'Exile.'

'Oh. That's not that bad. I was thinking, like, death or something.'

Te'rnu looked outraged. '*Death?* What good would that do anyone? That would be an awful punishment.'

'Yeah. I guess,' I replied. 'I was being paranoid, maybe.'

'Do not think exile is "not bad", however, Syl Raynor,' Te'rnu continued, his voice solemn. 'Imagine being cast out of the only world you have ever known. Imagine being thrown out there, into the great unknown, and knowing nobody and nothing. You would have to start your whole life again—because your last had ended. In a way, it is not wholly different from death.'

Point taken.

'Well,' I said. 'If it comes to that—and I'm sure it won't—at least you'll know me.'

Te'rnu smiled at the idea. 'It is nice to know this.'

We waited in silence—me unphased, Te'rnu worried, and Pr'atu practically soiling himself. I turned to the young one.

'It's OK, Pr'atu, they won't come down hard on you.'

'How do you know?' Pr'atu responded.

'We told them we coerced you into it, didn't we?'

'Yes,' the young Arellian replied, 'But how do *you*, as an off-worlder, know whether that will be enough?'

'It would be a terrible justice system if it didn't,' I answered.

The Elders didn't take long to deliberate, and returned to the room within a couple of minutes. This, I suspected, was not a good sign.

It was Elder Ra'ntu who stood to deliver the verdict—and the smirk on their face made it seem like they took great pleasure in doing so.

'We have reached a conclusion,' Ra'ntu announced, and what little murmuring was still taking place in the building came to an immediate halt. All eyes were on Ra'ntu.

Exactly as they liked it—all attention on them. Couldn't have anyone else upstaging them, could we?

'The off-worlder brought disquiet to our village. She brought with her rage, and an unwillingness to let us live our lives as we wish for them to be lived. She has disrespected the great Tradition, and so a punishment will be assigned to her.'

I laughed. What a ridiculous idea this was. 'I mean, there's not a huge amount you can make me do, is there? I could always just... walk away.'

'Then why haven't you?' the third Elder asked.

I shrugged. 'Guess I was curious.'

'And it has nothing to do with ensuring that Te'rnu is not punished too severely?' Ra'ntu asked, knowing eyes staring deep into mine. This wiped the smile from my face.

I couldn't formulate a smart retort in a reasonable time, and the absence of one was telling.

'Te'rnu,' Ra'ntu continued, 'Has again and again sought to undermine the fragile ecosystem of our village. Te'rnu cares little for the arrangement we have with the Iyr; the very generous deal by which the Iyr relieve us of our pain. If Te'rnu were to have their way, we would all end our lives in agony. It is my personal belief that if Te'rnu's presence in this village is continued to be tolerated, it would spell an end for Te'r'ok. For Te'rnu's crimes, a punishment *will* be given.'

I looked at my friend. His mouth hung agape, his skin pale.

'And, finally,' Ra'ntu went on, 'There is Pr'atu.'

Pr'atu rose from their seat for their verdict.

'The testimony given by both Te'rnu and the off-worlder seem to clear you of any wrongdoing.'

Pr'atu looked immediately relieved.

'However!' Ra'ntu continued. 'Should the given testimony ever be proven to be false, or otherwise inaccurate, we shall have to re-visit this decision. We will be keeping a close watch on your behaviour, young Arellian. For now, however, with your guilt unproven, you will receive no punishment.'

Pr'atu nodded. 'Thank you, Elder.'

'You may leave,' Elder Or'ane instructed Pr'atu.

This left just Te'rnu and I at the front bench.

'We have deemed that equal crimes deserve equal punishment,' Elder Ra'ntu announced. 'And with that in mind, we rule that you both shall be punished with exile.'

This sentence was uttered without any pause or emphasis, as though giving such a damning punishment meant nothing to

Ra'ntu. Te'rnu shrank into his seat, his face turning white.

'How the... fuck... is that an equal punishment?' I asked, astounded.

I'm getting really good at this swearing thing! Maybe I should try it more often. No, stop- Focus, Syl.

'This, here, Te'r'ok, that's Te'rnu's whole life! I'm just a visitor! Let's face it, I was going to leave soon anyway, and chances were that I wouldn't come back.'

'You wouldn't?' Ra'ntu asked.

'Are you kidding? No! There's a whole galaxy out there, and you think I'd want to come back to the one village that *you* live in?'

Whoops. Maybe too far. Dial it back.

'I'll happily leave and not come back if that's what you want— but Te'rnu should be able to stay.'

'Our decision is final,' Ra'ntu insisted.

Exasperated, I turned to Te'rnu, and began to plead with him. 'Come on, say something! Make your case! This is ridiculous.'

He only shook his head. 'There's no point. As they say: the decision is final. It always is.'

'You will be gone within the hour,' Ra'ntu instructed.

And then, the Elders, having apparently decided that the conversation was over, left the building.

Only Elder Or'ane stopped to look back. 'I am sorry, Te'rnu. If I had had my way...'

They trailed off, went silent for a moment.

'I am sorry,' Or'ane repeated.

10. One Person Can't Change A Galaxy

I sat at Te'rnu's side, hand placed on his arm, and hoped that this was considered a gesture of consolation on Z'h'ar, as it is on Terra.

'It's OK, Te'rnu, you're too good for here anyway,' I told him.

There was no response—no verbal or non-verbal sign that he had heard me. It was as though he had gone into shock.

I spent the majority of our allotted hour trying to get through to him, but nothing worked. He remained still, barely a sign of life in him.

Soon, the Elders came for us. A shadow loomed over the doorway as the Arellians blocked the light.

'It is time,' Ra'ntu announced, clearly taking great pleasure in informing us of this.

Do you want to be any more smug about it, maybe?

I tried to budge Te'rnu, to lead him out of the building—but he wouldn't move.

Before long, the stares of the Elder grew piercing. They began to advance on me. I could sense that they would next resort to physically removing Te'rnu and me from the village.

I had to give up. I stood and began to walk to the door.

Behind me, Te'rnu followed with his head held low, staring at the floor. Even in his hollow state, he finally recognised that he had no choice here.

We proceeded in silence, the two of us walking through the village as the rest of the inhabitants looked upon us. Pair after pair of sad eyes followed us—or, rather, followed Te'rnu.

We left the town without turning back, and I moved in the direction of the shuttle-bike. It was only two rotations previous that I had abandoned it in my sunstroke-inflicted haze, but it felt like a lifetime ago.

Te'rnu continued to follow, his head still hanging low, towards his chest.

'How we doing, there, buddy?' I asked him.

I got no verbal response from Te'rnu, but he did at least make eye contact with me. And then, eventually, he sighed. His sigh carried all the pain of a lifetime lost.

'I'm sorry, you know. That I convinced you to do this,' I told him. 'It was stupid, really. For a moment there, I thought we could learn something which would change your world, make things better for you guys. I really did think that.'

Te'rnu remained quiet, brow furrowed. I could sense that he was considering this thoroughly. I continued to proclaim my regret.

'But our plan was doomed before it even began, wasn't it? People can't change things, not really, not on their own. Life just works that way—it crushes you, puts you into a hopeless job, into a broken family, into an uninspiring existence. I should have remembered that.'

I shook my head, trying to rid myself of these depressing thoughts.

'Anyway,' I continued. 'I'm sorry.'

Te'rnu looked up at me. 'It is not your fault. At some point, I would have done it anyway. The truth... must always be known.'

I flashed Te'rnu a hopeful smile. 'I couldn't have said it better myself.'

My Arellian friend laid his eyes upon the abandoned shuttle-bike.

'Where are we going to go?'

We?

I paused for a moment. 'You're coming with me?'

Te'rnu shrugged. 'You said it yourself, back there, in the trial: you are the only person that I know, now. You are my only friend.'

He hesitated on this last point.

'You *are* my friend, right?' he followed up.

'Of course, Te'rnu. Of course I am,' I reassured him. 'But... are you sure you want to come with me? I won't be on Z'h'ar forever, and much less in the Wastelands...'

'There is nobody else I know,' Te'rnu repeated, his voice hollow.

I took a moment to process this. I couldn't abandon Te'rnu here, after he had saved me, after he had agreed to help me in that doomed mission. My case could wait; I had a friend in need.

'OK. Well, how about we visit another Arellian village? Maybe we can rest there, figure out our next move?'

And maybe you'll begin to realise that there are plenty of other places out there that you can call a home.

'OK,' Te'rnu replied.

I started up the shuttle-bike. 'So, erm...,' I began, 'Where *is* the next village?'

Te'rnu pointed to the west. 'Nu'r'ka. It is that way.'

'Alright, hop on,' I told him, doing just that myself.

He stood still, didn't move.

'You alright?' I prompted him. 'What's the hold-up?'

'What do I do?' Te'rnu asked, looking terrified by the prospect of sitting on a shuttle-bike.

'Just sit behind me, leg either side, like I am. And hold on to me—tight. So you don't fall off.'

Te'rnu, cautiously, did as instructed, sitting on the bike behind me and putting his arms around my torso in order to hold on.

'OK, great! I'm just gonna...'

I pulled Te'rnu's hands away from my breasts, where they seemed to have ended up, and moved them down to my belly.

'Perfect,' I assured him. 'Now keep holding tight, yeah?'

I started up the shuttle-bike's engine, and as it purred into life, I felt Te'rnu's grip tighten.

'It's OK, Te'rnu. It's perfectly safe.'

There was no reply.

I pulled on the accelerator and we sped west, undulating over the dunes in the early morning sun.

Before long, Te'rnu's arm stretched out to my right.

'There,' he said. 'It is Nu'r'ka.'

And indeed it was. The Arellian village sprawled out before us. It was bigger than Te'r'ok; there were more houses, more people. Most notably of all, the locals from Nu'r'ka seemed to be in possession of their own technology. Some carried transporter sonars, with which they were carrying their plentiful supply of food. Others spoke on radios to faraway villagers.

'It has changed,' Te'rnu commented.

'It didn't used to be like this? The size? And the radios?' I guessed.

'No,' he replied, a cautious tone to his voice, 'It did not.'

I pulled up outside the village, just past the last of the town's buildings, and something caught my eye.

A tall statue, made from the local orange rock, stood tall in the central square, next to Nu'r'ka's own Iyr beacon. Maybe this wouldn't have been striking in and of itself, but to me, it most certainly was.

The monument, as confirmed by the nameplate at the bottom, was of Leya Raynor.

My sister had been here. Here, on Z'h'ar. In Nu'r'ka.

Maybe it was about time I looked at her diary again; and at what little I had been able to decrypt.

The Diary of Leya Raynor

"Dear Diary"

Gu, 12e-05-2332

Dear Diary...

Is that a cliché, starting this like that? It feels like a cliché. Like I'm thirteen years old and I'm about to write about my crush who was mean to me in school today or something. No. I'm not doing that.

I'll start again.

Dear Reader....

Too formal?

Ah, fudge it. Who cares? I'll feel this out as I go.

I said my goodbye to Mum today. It was a "goodbye" rather than an "au revoir" because I don't know how long this journey is gonna take me. Could be weeks, could be years. Hopefully, I'll stop by on Terra every now and then if it ends up being years. It's not like I expect anything to happen to me or anything.

Mum didn't take it very well. The reason I'm going, that is. I mean, I didn't really expect that she would; last time she had any clue what Dad was doing, she got hooked on the 'Liks. I've sent Syl a message to stop by at home soon, to make sure Mum has support if need be. Can't have her relapsing.

My first destination was the planet *Gu*. It was the only place I could really remember Dad going on any regular occasion, so it made sense that I would start my search for him there. I had an address, which I took from an old diary of his. It was scrawled in the margins of it, like he was in a rush. That scribble had always felt important to me.

I went there as soon as I landed, not even bothering to try to find a place to stay. I only had a backpack with me, I should mention; I didn't pack much. Just a few changes of clothes, the basic sanitary items to keep me going, and a hair-sonar (I might not always be dressed perfectly on this trip, but I'll be darned before I have bad hair). Anything else that I *do* need, I can pick up as I go.

Sorry. I'm realising now how rambly this is all coming across. I'll make more of an effort from now on to write better. I never did well in Terran language class, after all.

See, there, I'm doing it again—going off on a tangent! I'll stop. Really, I'll stop this time. I'll make it read more clearly. Like you're reading an actual professional piece or something.

Right. Where was I?

I went straight to the address that was scribbled in the margins of the diary, letters clipped at the side of the page where the stylus crept off the pad. It was a small house, barely average in size by Gulien standards, that stood in the poorer outskirts of one of the cities.

I buzzed at the front gate and was immediately welcomed by a full-body scan. Head to toe, x-ray, sonar, the works. You name it, they had it. Clearly *this* was where all their money had gone. After taking a small sample of my blood, a message popped up on the screen:

Relative of Ira Raynor.

There it was: proof that I was on the right tracks! Without asking me any questions, the house's inhabitants granted me entry, and I walked in through the open gate.

I didn't know what I had really been expecting to be inside, but it wasn't this. The house was bustling with people, all with dour expressions on their faces, all dressed entirely in black. Of course, I just *had* to have been wearing a bright red coat at the time, so I could stand out like a sore thumb.

A young man came up to me, introduced himself as the son of the man who I had been looking for, and explained to me that his father has passed away just this morning.

Typical! I faff about for years before I start my search, and the man I begin with passes away on the very morning that I leave home. I kept this to myself, of course.

This wasn't my immediate reaction, I should add. I'm not a sociopath! I offered my sincerest condolences and then asked if there was anything I could do. There was indeed something I could do, it turned out: I could help with the U'kka run. Once the hot drinks were divvied out amongst the grieving family, the son sat me down and asked about the reason for my visit.

He seemed like a kind man, taking the time out of his day to ask about me, acting sincerely interested in what I had to say about my father, and how he might have known the deceased. The son confirmed this—he remembered my father visiting when he was a child. He told me that my father was always courteous towards him, occasionally brought him gifts, and always wore a smile. I had to check we were definitely talking about the same person.

The son showed me pictures. Of Dad. He really had been there, and it seemed as though he was, dare I say it, *chummy,* even, with the Gulien. In some of the pictures he even had an arm around the deceased's shoulders.

I pressed the son as much as I could about the nature of my father's visit, but he struggled to give me any information. He was too young, he said, to remember properly, but his sister might know. She was older back then, more likely to have had some clue about what was going on.

Of course, she wasn't around yet. She worked on Rykan (lucky her!) but was on her way over for the funeral already.

The son invited me to stay with him, until she arrived, as long as I didn't mind sleeping on a sofa. I suspected he liked the look of me, but maybe I was imagining things—he was grieving his father at the time, after all.

I made myself as useful as I could around the house, which mostly involved making U'kka, and waited for the sister to arrive with the information I was searching for.

11. All This Life Amongst The Stars

I rushed towards the statue in the centre of town, leaving Te'rnu behind at the shuttle-bike.

The heads of the local Arellians turned to look at me as I sprinted, but there was something different about their reactions here. In Te'r'ok, my Terran form had been enough to elicit gasps, stares of awe, even mouths left hanging agape. In Nu'r'ka, however, there was no wonder on the faces of the Arellians. They'd seen my type before—not just an off-worlder, apparently, but specifically a Terran. In place of awe, there was only confusion.

Why is this strange Terran rushing up to our statue with such a look on her face?

As I got closer to the monument of my sister, the smaller text on the plaque became more legible. Underneath Leya's name, it said:

"Saviour of Nu'r'ka"

Not a bad title.

I grabbed at the arm of a passing local, who flinched away and turned to look at me with wide eyes.

'Why...,' I started—and then realised I might have offended the Arellian. 'Sorry for grabbing you, I just wanted to... can I ask you something?'

Te'rnu appeared at my side, having rushed after me. The locals, who had been sporting such stiff and uncomfortable body language since I arrived, seemed to be relieved to see that I was travelling with a fellow Arellian. Their shoulders unclenched, their movements became more fluid.

'What is it that you would like to know?' the Arellian I had semi-assaulted asked me.

'Why... why do you have this statue?' I replied, still trying to get to grips with the concept of my sister being here—and on top of that, being their "saviour".

'Leya is our saviour,' the Arellian replied, as though that was enough of an answer.

Yeah, I can see that from the plaque.

'But... how? Why? What did she do?'

The local Arellian looked at me with a furrowed brow, as though I was asking a stupid question.

'She saved our town.'

Oh my god...

'Yes, but *how* did she save your town?'

'By renegotiating our deal. With the Iyr.'

Suddenly the improved technology and the abundance of food in Nu'r'ka was beginning to make sense.

'She helped you? Why? I can't say I've ever known my sister to put much effort in-'

The local Arellian's grew wide.

'You are the sister of Leya Raynor?!' the local exclaimed, with sheer joy on their face.

Other locals immediately stopped what they were doing and turned to face me, only now adopting the same look of awe that I had received in Te'r'ok.

The village began murmuring excitedly, and there was a very perceivable sense of delight in the air. I could even hear an Arellian using their radio to spread the news to others. It was almost like a queen had come to visit.

I felt like a con artist. I was no queen, I was an underpaid private investigator, who hadn't ever *really* helped anyone in any meaningful way. In fact, I was only even here because a number of unfortunate circumstances had conspired to put me here.

The Arellian I had first spoken to approached me with their arms spread wide.

'Oh, err,' I started, 'What's happening here?'

And then their arms closed gently around me.

'It is called a "hug". Your sister, the Saviour, taught it to us.'

Were we talking about the same Leya Raynor?

I hugged the Arellian back. It was only polite.

Once the Arellian let go of me, another approached to do the same. Over and over it went, hug after hug. I received more displays of affection within these five minutes than I had in my entire life to date—although, admittedly, that problem was largely due to my bad choices in romantic partners.

Towards the end of these five minutes, I found myself being hugged by Te'rnu.

'What you doing there, buddy?' I asked him.

'Oh, I, err...,' he began to reply. 'I thought we were *all* doing it.'

I laughed and hugged him back.

One of the older locals, after completing the supposedly traditional display of affection, turned to the rest of the now large crowd, and announced, 'Tonight, we feast!'

I insisted that Te'rnu and I help prepare this feast, and the locals lauded my family's generosity. I must come from a kind bloodline, they told me. I denied this and told them I actually came from a bloodline of unsuccessful artists. This response was a mistake—as it meant that I spent more time describing the galactic art industry and the economics surrounding it than I did actually helping with the cooking.

Te'rnu, on the other hand, was elsewhere, collecting raw materials for the fire with the stronger locals, as well as helping decant a "special surprise liquid" which the village was eager to share with us. There were not eager, however, to tell us exactly what it was—we would just have to taste it, we were told.

I was conscious that the past day or so had been a real detour from the reason I had originally come to the Arellian Wastelands—to find Melonaitopila. But the discovery that my sister had been here was too much of an opportunity to pass up. If it was a toss-up between finding the target (and keeping my job) and finding my sister, well, my family just had to come first. I swore to myself that once the feast was over—and I had sufficiently questioned the entire village about my sister's time here—I would return to the task at hand.

The feast itself began in much the same way as dinner in Te'r'ok had. All the villagers sat in a circle, with a designated few serving the food—this seemed to be the way it was done in the Arellian wastelands. In Nu'r'ka, however, the town was populous enough that there were several circles, with the inside circles on lower ground—so that all participants still had an equal view.

The Arellian who announced the feast, who I had correctly determined was one of Nu'r'ka's Elders, instructed me and Te'rnu to sit in the central circle, right next to the now blazing fire. This seemed like it was the prime placement, reserved for anyone held in high esteem—but, not being used to this warmer climate, I could really have used being further away from the fire. I kept this preference to myself, and hoped nobody would notice—or failing that, hoped nobody would care—about the sweat building up on my back.

The food, here, in Nu'r'ka, was absolutely incredible. It was similar in consistency to the food in Te'r'ok, but the flavour here was so extraordinary you could even taste it on the air floating up from the bowl. I tucked in, hungrily, and was pleased to see my bowl get refilled several times.

I could get used to this whole 'being treated like a queen' thing, actually.

When I had eaten all the food that I could possibly stomach, I returned to the matter at hand: it was time to ask about my sister. I turned to the Elder next to me, leaving Te'rnu alone, licking his lips as he ate his meal.

'I was hoping to ask: what exactly did Leya negotiate for you that she is revered so much?' I asked.

'Have you seen other Arellian settlements?' the Elder asked. 'I say this not out of malice—we were once like them—but they have little food or resources, or even time for themselves. Their existence is a basic one.'

'And now...'

'And now we have more food than we know what to do with.'

'Hence the feast,' I added.

'And,' the Elder continued, 'We have some of the Iyr's spare technology, which Leya taught us to fix, to maintain. Some of us are so well-versed in these devices that they are even improving them. As far as I am aware, we are the first Arellian village to have an Elder of Technology.'

They pointed across the circle to an Arellian who seemed to be wearing some sort of device on their head.

'That is them, over there.'

Yeah. With the thing on their head. Got it.

'All of this... we would not have if not for your sister. She came here, she saw how we were living. Then she spent time here, understanding our lifestyle. Once she realised that it was the Tradition which was stifling our lives, she went to the Iyr, demanded a negotiation.'

'And how did she convince them?' I asked.

'We know not of this. These negotiations were done in the Stronghold, where we are—still, even now—not allowed to travel.'

'You don't have an inkling, even?'

'What is this? "Inkling"?'

'You don't have any idea? Whatsoever?' I asked, rephrasing.

'If we did, we would tell you. We would tell *anything* to the sister of our Saviour.'

Leya being called a saviour was really starting to get annoying. *I could be a saviour too if I wanted to.*

'So... her negotiation means that you don't pay tribute any more? You just keep all your food to yourself?'

'Why?' the Elder asked. 'Do you think that is selfish?'

'No, not at all. As far as I'm concerned, if you guys are farming it, putting all the hard work in, then you should be keeping it.'

The Elder smiled. 'Good. We don't keep all of it, however. When the Mutation begins-'

The Arellian cut themselves off.

'You know of the Mutation?' they asked.

'I do,' I assured them.

'When the Mutation begins, and the Iyr come for the dying, we pay the Iyr the tribute then. But only then.' They paused, grinned at me. 'You are lucky. To have family like this.'

I pursed my lips. 'I don't.'

Te'rnu, now finished his food, turned to listen in to the conversation.

'You do not?' the Elder asked.

'I haven't seen her in years. Nobody knows where she's gone.

In fact, we assumed she'd been dead, she had been gone so long.'

There was a moment of silence, the two Arellians acknowledging my pain.

'I am sorry she is missing,' Te'rnu offered me.

Another silence.

'Do you...,' I began. 'Do you know anything? About where she might have gone?'

'We know little. We know she was looking for someone, as you are doing for her.'

'Looking for someone? Was it our Dad?' I asked.

The Elder shook their head. 'I am afraid we know not. It could have been, but she did not say.'

'So that's why she was here? She was looking for them on Z'h'ar?' I pressed.

'On our planet? No. She was here for something else.'

'Do you know what it was?' I asked.

The Elder shook their head once again. 'I wish we could do more to assist you in your search.'

Te'rnu put his hand on my arm in an attempt to console me, copying as I had done to him after the trial.

Suddenly, an Elder approached us. Behind them, four Arellians carried a huge metal container.

'Is this the liquid?' Te'rnu asked.

The Elder, in answer, announced, 'There was one other gift that your sister presented us with: knowledge. Specifically, she taught unto us the secrets of distillation. I present to you, Arellian Gin!'

Yep. It was definitely my Leya who had been here.

I burst out laughing—to the confusion of everyone around me.

'She always loved her gin, that one,' I informed them.

They responded with a faint smile, as though still not quite understanding what there was to laugh about, and then began to pour the gin into smaller bowls.

Most—if not all—of the Arellians were served the gin. They drank happily—even the children. Whereas most races might frown on giving alcohol to children, Leya clearly hadn't parted that wisdom onto the Arellians, and it seemed were yet to learn this lesson for themselves.

I watched as Te'rnu took a hesitant sip. As he tasted it, his eyes widened.

'I like this!' he announced, and other Arellians around him cheered in response. A wide smile spread across his face, momentarily replacing that melancholy expression he had been sporting since the trial.

We drank long into the night, and it was my first experience seeing the Arellians actually loosen up a little—Te'rnu in particular. The joy of these villagers was contagious; a night of drinking, dancing, and making stupid jokes had me feeling like I was a teenager again.

'It's funny!' I told a passing Arellian.

'What is?' they replied.

'You give people, of any race, alcohol, and their evenings become this. No matter how proud, or cold, or... *whatever* a species is—when alcohol is involved, they learn to love a good party.'

The Arellian smiled politely in response; clearly this wasn't so funny to them. Maybe you needed to have had seen more of the galaxy.

Te'rnu grabbed me by the arm and insisted I joined him and a group of locals in dancing. They taught me their moves and laughed when I taught them some old Terran classics: the chicken, the robot, flossing. They found the chicken particularly funny—which was kinda weird, because birds didn't exist on Z'h'ar.

Many of the locals partnered off over the course of the night, leaving a smaller and smaller crowd dwindling behind.

As is always the way, eventually the plentiful supply of alcohol was no longer enough to keep my energy levels up. I soon found myself lying down, on the bare ground, in front of the monument to my sister.

I stared up at the stars. The constellations were so different on Z'h'ar; many clusters of stars were dotted about the night sky, some even bright enough to cast faint shadows.

Te'rnu's face suddenly blocked my view as he stood over me.

'Are you OK down there?' he asked.

I said nothing, just waved frantically at him to join me.

He didn't take the hint. 'Why are you lying on the ground? There are beds for us.'

'Lie down, Te'rnu, for god's sake!'

'What is "god's"?'

I shook my head. 'Remind me to tell you another time.'

Te'rnu laid down on the floor next to me, and too looked up at the stars.

'You have pretty stars here,' I told him.

'Would you like me to tell you about them?' he asked.

'Yeah, go on then.'

Te'rnu pointed up at a particularly bright cluster. 'Those, there. We use those for navigation. When we used to travel back to Te'r'ok from the farm, late at night, we just followed them. The Returners, we called them—they will always bring you home.'

He took a moment to collect his thoughts. Perhaps the memory of Te'r'ok was getting to him.

Te'rnu pointed at another set of stars.

'And those, do you see a face?'

I grunted in acknowledgement.

'We say the stars are smiling at us. If we can see the Smiling

Stars in the night's sky on the first day of spring, we know that the crops will grow strong that year.'

'What are your favourites?' I asked Te'rnu.

'I never really had any.'

'No?'

'No. For me, I mostly dreamt of adventuring amongst them, as the spacemen do. But I was always told: that is not the life I was given.'

'That's just the thing, though, Te'rnu. Nobody gets to tell you what kind of life you have to live. Maybe you'll be the first Arellian, out there, travelling the cosmos.'

We said nothing for a few more moments and simply stared up at the sky, appreciating its beauty.

'Earlier today, Syl, you said something.'

'Oh, no. Since getting drunk, you mean? What did I say?' I responded.

'No, before that. Before we arrived in Nu'r'ka. You told me that one person cannot hope to change the world.'

'Yeah, I remember.'

Te'rnu gestured at the monument to Nu'r'ka's saviour—to Leya.

'Maybe one person cannot change our world, but they can still make things better: village by village, person by person. Your sister is proof of that.'

I said nothing.

'Maybe,' Te'rnu continued. 'You would consider helping *me*?'

'How would I help you?' I asked.

'I would like to continue our investigation. I would like to know, for certain, whether we Arellians can live on... beyond our Mutation. Would you help me find the truth?'

I stared up at the looming statue.

Saviour of Nu'r'ka.

'OK, Te'rnu. I'll help. To hell with changing *the* world—let's just try and change *your* world.'

'What is "hell"?' Te'rnu asked.

12. They Don't Have Aspirin On Z'h'ar

rgh!' Te'rnu shouted.

I jumped to my feet. 'What is it?!' I called out to him.

I looked around to find Te'rnu on the floor, clutching his head.

'No!' he screamed. 'The Mutation! It has started!'

Other Arellians in town watched on—but didn't seem too worried. This definitely wasn't the same reaction as the locals had had in Te'r'ok. But maybe that was because...

'Where's the pain?' I asked Te'rnu.

'In my head!' he cried out. 'It is awful! And my mouth feels so dry!'

I was starting to get a clue about what was happening here.

'Isn't the pain supposed to start in your groin? What's happening down there?'

'My groin is fine! It is my head that is hurting!'

'Hmm.'

I stood up, grabbed a bowl of water for him.

'Here,' I told Te'rnu, 'Drink this.'

He sipped timidly at the water bowl that I gripped in my

hands, much as I had done when I had first arrived in Te'r'ok.

'Yeah... I think we're gonna have to get you some hair of the dog, buddy,' I said.

'Dog hair? What will I need that for?'

'Not... not actual dog hair. It's an expression: "hair of the dog that bit you". It means-'

'No,' Te'rnu replied, shaking his head (and then clutching it again when doing so caused him pain), 'I have never been bitten by a dog. Animals tend to like me.'

'Oi, listen! It *means...*,' I repeated, 'Having more of whatever ails you.'

'But it's the Mutation!' Te'rnu cried out.

'It's not the Mutation, mate,' I responded, resisting the urge to laugh about it. 'You just drank too much last night.'

'Too much? Too much gin?'

'Yes. You're hungover.'

Te'rnu moaned. 'Well, I do not like it.'

'No. You wouldn't.'

'This is why you passed out, back near Te'r'ok?'

I nodded. 'Yeah. Partially.'

'I understand now,' Te'rnu replied, now no longer clutching at his head but instead using his hands to block the sunlight from hitting his eyes.

I laughed. 'Oh, Te'rnu... You won't be doing *that* again in a hurry, will you?'

Did I really just say that? Was I turning into my mother?

I remembered Leya and I sneaking some of Mum's wine when we were younger. Or rather, I remember us stealing some of her "painting juice"—as she would call it. Once Mum had gone to sleep, Leya and I took turns swigging from the bottle. I didn't really like it at the time, but my sister seemed to, so I pretended I was having fun too.

Was my current level of alcohol consumption in any way related to that night?

Leya and I awoke in the morning, complaining of flu symptoms. Mum, understandably, was shocked—especially because the flu virus had been eradicated over a hundred years earlier. It didn't take her long to find the empty bottle of wine hidden under my bed.

My Mum held Leya and I's hair, as we spent the day throwing up into the toilet and a large bucket, respectively. I assumed that I was assigned the bucket simply because I was younger, and not because there was any favouritism going on. Maybe there was, though, looking back on it now.

'No,' Te'rnu replied. 'I will not. I'm never drinking again.'

'Yeah, we've all said that one before.'

My friend vomited up last night's dinner on to my sister's feet. I couldn't help but enjoy the symbolism—just a little bit.

He moaned. 'Ohhh... they will not like that.'

I grabbed a nearby bowl, put it next to him, and repositioned Te'rnu's head so that it was over this container rather than this town's monument to their Saviour. Thankfully, Te'rnu didn't have hair he would need someone to hold up—I didn't massively fancy that job.

'Yeah, don't worry, I'll clear it up,' I told Te'rnu, feigning exasperation.

I grabbed a spare bit of cloth that seemed to have been left behind after last night's feast, and used it to wipe the vomit off the statue—hopefully, nobody was missing a headscarf or anything. I tossed the cloth behind some crates—just in case.

Seeing that the container of gin still had some remnants at the bottom of it, I scooped some up. Some of the alcoholic fumes wafted upwards into my nostrils.

Whew! Even I didn't fancy any of that right now.

I offered it to Te'rnu, who recoiled, like I had, at the smell of it.

'No!' he moaned.

'Yes!' I countered.

'I cannot drink it!' he insisted.

'You can, it'll make you feel better.'

Te'rnu sighed. 'OK. Just a tiny bit, though.'

'That's all I'm asking you to drink.'

My Arellian friend sipped a little of the alcohol and immediately vomited again. He groaned.

'OK. Maybe a little too early for that,' I told him. 'We'll try again later when your stomach is settled. Just keep sipping that water, will you?'

There was no reply. Te'rnu sat with his head in his hands.

'I said: will you keep sipping that water?'

'Yes,' he groaned.

'Good.'

I left Te'rnu to his own devices for a while. Walking slowly, so that my own hangover wouldn't lead me to collapse again, I headed towards the top of a nearby hill.

From its peak, I could see the Iyr capital in the distance. The nearby sun rose just to the right of it, from where I was standing, and its rays reflected off the taller buildings. In this light, the city was beautiful.

I sat down for a while, watching distant ships land in the capital's shipyards, and occasionally turning my attention to the Arellian village below. The locals were beginning to rise, and, like Te'rnu, they weren't in the best of states.

It was just like Leya to forget to teach moderation.

Over the course of the day, the Arellians slowly returned to their usual selves—their bodies becoming less hunched, their voices becoming less raspy, and their moods becoming less irritable.

When I felt that Te'rnu had recovered enough to have a serious conversation, I approached him about what we'd discussed the night before—about how I could help him.

I coaxed him part-way up the hill, away from prying ears.

'So what's the plan?' I asked.

'The plan?'

'Yeah, the plan. I told you I'd help, didn't I? What's the plan?'

'There is no plan,' Te'rnu clarified. 'I need help with that bit too.'

I sighed. 'OK, right. Well, then, let's start brainstorming. What is it we want to achieve?'

'We want to know the truth about the Mutation. And, perhaps, any other secrets that the Iyr are hiding.'

'Great! So...,' I asked, 'If we could do anything at all, go anywhere we wanted, how would we find this out?'

'I suppose we would go to Central Command. If there are files on the Arellians anywhere, it would be there.'

'Central Command?' I said, thinking of my case—of the diplomat's daughter that had been taken by the Iyr. 'Is that the same place they would have taken Melonaitopila?'

Te'rnu shrugged. 'It is likely. But getting inside would be impossible for us.'

'Why?' I asked, more to play devil's advocate than anything else.

My friend looked at me incredulously. '"Why?" We... we are an Arellian. And a Terran.'

'But what if we weren't?'

'You wish us to... change species?' Te'rnu asked, looking no less sceptical than before.

'No, obviously not. But how would they know what we are

121

under a mechsuit?'

Te'rnu's eyebrows raised so high, I thought they were going to fly off his face. 'You want us to *steal* mechsuits?!'

'What, you have moral qualms about stealing from the people who have been stealing from you your *entire life*?'

'What do you mean?'

I stood up and began to pace, using my hands to gesticulate, punctuating my argument. 'I mean... if you're right about the Mutation, then the Iyr really aren't doing you any favours by taking Arellians away. So what are the tributes if not thievery?'

Te'rnu said nothing.

'I'm not telling you anything you don't already know, here, Te'rnu.'

He began to nod. 'OK. You are right. If they can steal from us, then we can steal from them.'

'There's the Arellian I know!' I said, voice raised with excitement.

'I know where they keep them,' Te'rnu followed up.

'Even better!' I cried out. 'Where?'

'There is a guard barracks. The Iyr took me there a few times— when they caught me in the city. It is near the gate. I can get us there.'

Satisfied that this plan was coming together, I took a seat back next to Te'rnu, and stared out onto the village.

'We can do this, Te'rnu. We can find out the truth, and then...,' I gestured to the town in front of us. 'All their lives will be different.'

Te'rnu nodded, brow furrowed.

'There's something else that I'd like to do, while we're in there...,' I began.

'What? As well as finding Melonaitopila?'

'Yeah. You remember this?'

I pulled Leya's journal from my bag, put it in Te'rnu's hands. He brushed the sand from the front and inspected it, fascinated by the technology.

'Yes... you said it was your sister's diary?'

'I'd like to decrypt it. Well, I'd like to decrypt the part of it that looks like it's in the Iyr's language. I tried, back at the outpost, but... the encryption is too complicated, it couldn't handle it. I figure... the truth about the Mutation—if it exists—will be on their central computer libraries. If we can access that, then we should be able to decrypt the journal at the same time.'

Te'rnu shrugged, eyes vacant. 'Sure.'

Oh yeah, never used a computer before. Note to self: dial back the tech-talk around Te'rnu.

'It sounds like... we have a plan, then?'

'Yes,' Te'rnu replied, a slight smile on his face. 'I think we do. At this time tomorrow...'

'You could know the truth about the Mutation,' I finished for him. 'And I could save a young woman's life, save my job, and maybe work out where my sister is. Wouldn't be bad for a day's work, would it?'

Te'rnu grinned—fully this time, his brilliantly white teeth catching the sun.

'It would not be bad at all,' he said.

We watched the villagers of Nu'r'ka in silence for a while. They went about their usual business, some cleaning up the feast of the night before, others simply going off to work. I let the sun wash over me, and mentally prepared myself for the day that was about to come.

⇥

We firmed up the details of the plan over the next few hours—and then waited until nightfall. Te'rnu had told me that we wouldn't stand a chance of getting into the guard barracks undetected if we went during the day. What's more, at night, the number of guards on duty would be minimal—most would be at home at this time, he had previously discovered.

Even at night, however, Te'rnu had often been caught. We could only hope that this wasn't one of those times—an Arellian sneaking through the streets was one thing, but being caught breaking into the barracks would be so much worse.

We said our goodbyes to the town of Nu'r'ka and told them we would be back to visit soon. It seemed as though they had enjoyed our company—*any excuse for a party, right?*—even though both Te'rnu and I had potentially made fools of ourselves in our drunken states.

We headed off into the night, Te'rnu's arms gripping me tightly as we took the shuttle-bike back towards the stronghold. When we were close, I slowed to allow him to jump off, and I continued on to return the rented bike. I definitely wasn't going to risk the overtime fees out here, not after all my previous encounters with the abrasive Iyr.

I was pleased to see that there was nobody at the stall at this time of night, and so I would be able to avoid any irritating conversations with the local merchant. Having parked and locked my shuttle-bike up with the rest, and leaving a hastily scribbled note on it, I walked back into the wastelands to meet up with Te'rnu.

'How did it go?' Te'rnu asked me.

'Nobody around. I just left it there.'

'Will they know it is yours?'

'That's why I left a note.'

Te'rnu nodded, small talk complete, and led us towards the stronghold's walls.

'The gate's that way, Te'rnu,' I reminded him.

Te'rnu shook his head. 'We are not going in through the gate.

They would catch us that way. I have another way in.'

I said nothing, putting my faith in Te'rnu's knowledge of the capital, and continued to follow him through the darkness.

We weaved through the gaps in the floodlights, taking our time so as not to be spotted—until we came to a small, rusty, grated entrance to some kind of tunnel.

'What is it?' I asked as Te'rnu pulled the grate away from it, allowing us entry.

'The sewers,' Te'rnu replied.

I nodded. 'Of course it is.'

I cursed myself for not wearing thicker shoes when I had left the hotel a few nights earlier. That said, who could have known that a trip to a bar would have ended up like this?

We squeezed into the tunnel and crept down it. I was conscious of the water level increasing with every step.

Yes, 'water level'. Let's pretend this foul brown liquid is water. Lovely refreshing water. Yum.

Thankfully, before long, we reached an access point. Te'rnu, giving me a nod, began to climb up.

'I *told* you it was no great distance,' Te'rnu said.

'No you didn't,' I replied.

'Oh. I meant to.'

He signalled for me to be quiet, and then, slowly, as quietly as possible, he opened the hatch. Through the minutest of gaps, Te'rnu watched, waiting for the path to clear. It took some time, but eventually, sure enough, he was able to open the door, and we climbed out into a quiet backstreet.

'So this is how you always get in, huh?' I asked.

Te'rnu responded by shh-ing me. 'No time to speak.'

He waved me over to the cover of a large waste bin, and we crouched until the road was clear.

'This way,' Te'rnu whispered, before rushing quietly to a gap between the buildings.

We continued like this for a while—me struggling to keep my trap shut, and Te'rnu masterfully navigating us through the winding alleys of the Iyr stronghold. Finally, we came to the back entrance of a building bearing some of the Iyr's symbols, and Te'rnu turned to face me.

'This is it. This is the guard barracks.'

'Lovely,' I replied, 'Last chance, then—want to back out?'

Te'rnu took a moment to consider and then shook his head.

'You sure? If they catch us…' I trailed off—and left the result to his imagination.

'I am sure,' he replied. 'This is it. This is what my life has been heading towards.'

'Good answer.'

When the coast was clear, we crept up to the back door, and Te'rnu pulled on it.

It didn't budge.

'It is locked,' he told me.

'Yeah, I assumed.'

Te'rnu stared down at the ground, a look of deep concentration on his face. Then, he looked around at the exterior wall.

'Ah,' he said.

Next to the door, down by the ground, was a small metal grate. I could see exactly where this was headed.

Te'rnu pulled on the grate, and it fell to the floor with a clang. Terrified that we had alerted an Iyr to our presence, we both looked around, terrified.

But there was nobody in sight.

Te'rnu crouched to get into the now-open ventilation shaft.

'First creeping through sewers, and now crawling through air vents. You do know how to have a good time, don't you?'

My friend ignored this throwaway comment and gestured for me to quickly enter the ventilation behind him.

If Z'h'ar as a planet was hot, then it was nothing compared to this particular building's ventilation shaft.

Oh, boy. And I haven't even put deodorant on in three days.

Hot, humid air blasted us in the face as we crawled, as quietly as we could, through the enclosed space. Te'rnu began to steam ahead, as he was less affected by the heat than me. I was disappointed when Te'rnu rushed straight past the first possible exit.

'Te'rnu!' I whispered after him.

He peered over his shoulder as best he could in this limited space, and eyes widened when he saw me.

'It is too hot?'

'Yeah...,' I barely managed to croak.

He nodded—and then crawled backwards to get a look through the first grate.

'I do not see anyone...,' he mumbled.

'Think you can get this grate off without it crashing to the floor?' I asked.

Te'rnu shrugged.

'That doesn't fill me with confidence.'

With his delicate fingers, the Arellian pried the edge of the grate away from the shaft... and promptly lost his grip on it.

A clanging sound echoed around the hallway as it crashed to the floor.

'I dropped it,' Te'rnu clarified.

I pursed my lips. 'Yes.'

Quickly realising that being crammed into a small confined ventilation shaft didn't give us the best chances in a fight, I instructed Te'rnu to jump out.

Apparently adept in the art of covert operations all of a

sudden, he dropped silently to the ground and took cover in the nearest room.

I took a quick look at the drop. It wasn't far, maybe two and a half metres, and would put me in the middle of the barracks' central hallway. It was a long, narrow room with many doorways at its perimeter

I dropped, slightly more clumsily than my partner in crime, and grabbed the wall to catch my balance.

Behind me, I heard the familiar *whooom* of a phase weapon being started up.

Uh-oh.

'Stop!' an Iyr's voice shouted at me.

I slowly raised my hands and turned to face the Iyr whose trigger finger would determine if I lived or died.

13. Mechsuits: The Top Trend From Z'h'ar Fashion Week Spring/Summer 2337

Standing in front of me, phase rifle armed and ready to fire, was the Head of Guard. The red stripe on their helmet glistened under the neon lights.

'I know *you*!' the Iyr declared.

'Yeah? I know me too, so what?' I replied.

The Iyr paused. I couldn't see under their helmet, of course, but they almost seemed taken aback. After all, taking people aback *was* a speciality of mine.

Out of the corner of my eye, I could see an alarmed Te'rnu sneaking away. I did my best not to glance at him, so I wouldn't give his position away.

'What are you doing in here?' the Iyr demanded.

'I came to report a crime,' I replied.

'What?'

'A crime. I've come to report one.'

'You came… *here* for this?'

I feigned confusion. 'Well, you are the city's *guards* are you not?'

Another pause; longer, this time.

'Do you take pleasure in irritating me?' the Head of Guard asked. 'You disturb on our first meeting, and then you break into my place of work? Is it *me* that you are after?'

I forced a giggle, flashed the Iyr a smile, and did my best to gaze longingly at them. 'Do you want it to be?'

'No! Stop this!' the Iyr demanded, getting increasingly frustrated. 'I demand that you tell me why you are here.'

'You're all business, aren't you? I quite like that in a-'

'Tell me why you are here!' The Iyr aimed down the scope of their phaser.

'OK!' I replied, putting my hands up in the air to express my defeat. 'OK. I'll tell you.'

I took a breath.

'Do I need to have my hands up in the air? It's just I get pins and needles if I leave them up too long, and that's uncomfortable, and-'

The Iyr guard bashed me in the face with the butt of their rifle.

I fell to the floor—and tried to catch myself. My right hand slipped on the fresh patch of blood that my now-broken nose had so recently created. In a daze, I tried to blink my vision back into focus.

'What the…'

'I will *not* take any more of this from you. Tell me why you are here!' the Iyr screamed.

'I'm here to cast more of them aspersions, I guess,' I muttered, blood splattering from my mouth.

Now that my arms were no longer held in the air to signal my innocence, I—as subtly as I could—pulled back my right sleeve and prepared to activate my EMP.

'You think you are going to convince me that we, the *Iyr*, are in the wrong, here?'

'Wait, what? What are you talking about? What might you be in the-' I began, only to be interrupted by a roar erupting from the next room.

Te'rnu jumped out at the Head of Guard, swinging a long, metal pipe above his head.

Te'rnu brought his weapon crashing down with a crack into the Head of Guard's head. Sparks flew from the damaged helmet, causing the Iyr to cry with pain, before dropping to the floor. He looked up at me with wide, terrified eyes.

'Thanks, Te'rnu.'

He remained frozen, looking down at the Iyr and then at the pipe in his hands.

'It's OK, Te'rnu, it's OK,' I reassured him, holding my hand to my bleeding nose. 'You just did what you had to.'

He gulped, looking up at me, and realised I was injured. 'Are you OK?'

'Yeah,' I told him, trying to sound convincing, 'Just a broken nose. Nothing a med-sonar can't fix in two minutes.'

Te'rnu looked on at me as I held my jacket against my nose, trying to stop the bleeding.

'You are sure?' he asked.

I nodded, and Te'rnu instead turned his attention to the guard, nudging them. 'Do you think they are alive?'

'I don't know if we should stick around to find out.'

Te'rnu nodded, and we hurried up the hallway in search of the armoury—and the prized mechsuits.

'You can be very annoying when you want to be,' Te'rnu commented as we searched.

'Thanks,' I replied, voice muffled by the cloth across my face,

'I pride myself on it.'

We soon came across a room that housed three of the suits. It didn't *feel* like an armoury. In fact—between the desk and chair—it actually felt more like an office. I noticed an electronic frame on the desk and picked it up.

In the display was a family photo; two Iyr with their arms around one another, gazing at the camera. The couple each wore a mechsuit, so it was hard to tell exactly what was going on in the pictures, but it felt to me like a tender moment. The Iyr on the left, I noticed, had that same red stripe on their helmet—it was the Head of Guard.

I prayed that we hadn't killed them, that we hadn't deprived someone of their partner. I couldn't handle that kind of guilt.

Putting the frame back down on the desk, I turned to face Te'rnu. He had wasted no time in getting into one of the suits. Each mechanical limb hung loosely around his body, like a kid in their father's top.

'Doesn't look like it's fitting you very well, huh?'

Te'rnu frowned, looked down at the suit, and tried to move his legs. He had no such luck.

'I believe it is switched off,' he clarified, before pressing the very obvious red rectangular button on the chest area—one that I had been itching to press since the moment I had noticed it, all of half a second ago.

The suit jumped into life, adapting in size to fit Te'rnu's form with all the wondrous whizzes and whooshes that you would expect from a powered mechsuit. Once the helmet attached itself to Te'rnu's head, I could see that same red stripe marking this suit too. Either this was one of the Head of Guard's spares, or that decoration wasn't so rare as I had initially thought.

'How is it?' I asked Te'rnu.

He wiggled his limbs about, trying to get a better feel for the suit.

'Surprisingly comfortable,' he replied.

'Can it do anything fun?' I asked, remembering that the guidebook had told me that these suits were often upgraded with interesting features.

'There is a button on the viewscreen called "instant kill". Should I activate it?'

'No!' I replied instantly. 'At least... definitely not while I'm standing in front of you, thank you very much.'

'What about "incapacitate"?'

'Are you serious?' I asked. 'Are you trying to hurt me, Te'rnu?'

I heard a snickering from inside the suit. 'I am joking, Syl. I have noticed you like jokes. Was I wrong?'

I smiled, shook my head. 'No... you're not wrong. But maybe we need to work on your sense of humour. Is there a button for that in there?'

A pause.

'No, I don't think so.'

A longer pause.

'Oh,' Te'rnu murmured when he realised that I was not being entirely serious.

I flashed him a grin, nodded, and then tried to get into one of the mechsuits myself.

Instant kill? Incapacitate? This was going to be bloody amazing.

I slipped into the suit as Te'rnu had, and keenly pressed at the button.

Nothing happened.

'What is going on?' Te'rnu asked. 'Is it broken?'

'I don't know.'

I pressed the button again.

A voice from inside the suit announced, 'Incompatible biology detected.'

Damn.

'I guess it doesn't take Terrans,' I said, after a deep sigh.

'What are we going to do? Our plan was dependent on us having disguises. If you still look Terran...'

I flattened my lips. 'I know. Erm...'

I paused for a moment. My now-suited Arellian friend stared silently at me, mechanical red eyes glowing at me in the dim light.

'I could be your prisoner?' I suggested.

'How would that work?'

'You grab a phaser—must be one around here somewhere—and-'

'I could take the one from the Iyr we knocked unconscious.'

'Perfect. And then you lead me back to Central Command?'

After a moment of contemplation for the Arellian, he nodded. 'And if anyone asks... I have been ordered to bring you in.'

I bit my lip. 'I mean... it's a classic ploy, and that must be for a reason. Think it'll work?'

'I think it is the only plan we have,' he grumbled.

'Fair point.'

With the possibility that more guards could return to the barracks at any moment, we wasted little more time; stopping only to stuff the Head of Guard's body in the corner of a storeroom.

'Do you think we should...,' Te'rnu began to ask, gesturing at the Iyr's helmet.

I shook my head. 'The more time we spend here, the greater our chances of being caught. If everything goes to plan, then...'

'...Then we shall know everything anyway,' Te'rnu finished for me. 'OK. Let us continue.'

We slipped out the back door of the guard barracks and made our way towards our final destination: Central Command.

⇥▷

The impressive cubic building soon loomed over us—as, indeed, it did most things in the Iyr capital. Te'rnu stopped for a moment, stunned, when he first noticed it.

'You can't be stopping to admire the view now that you're an Iyr,' I told him. 'They see this every day.'

'It is bigger than it looks from the Wastelands.'

'Yep, that's generally how perspective works. Come on—we should hurry.'

Te'rnu and I assumed the "law enforcement and prisoner" formation—me walking in front, Te'rnu walking behind, phase rifle pointed in my direction.

'Just make sure you leave the safety on, eh?' I asked Te'rnu—and then realised that I would do well to actually explain the concept of a "safety" to him before he accidentally shot me.

We approached the main entrance to see that it was being guarded by two armed Iyr. I could feel Te'rnu's pace slow behind me, the reality of the danger he was putting himself in now being realised.

As we reached the main door, Te'rnu prepared to tout his reason for bringing me in.

'I am here to-'

The Iyr guard waved us through.

'Oh,' Te'rnu whispered. 'I see.'

'Rifle on the rack there,' the guard reminded him. Te'rnu responded with a curt nod, placed the phaser down by the Iyr, and turned to me.

He paused for a moment before grabbing me by the wrists and twisting them behind my back.

I played along—put up a little struggle, but essentially let him do it.

'Sorry,' Te'rnu whispered in my ear.

'Don't be,' I replied, 'At least, not so audibly.'

Te'rnu pretended to force me up the stairs in the main atrium, which led to a series of long, narrow hallways. We proceeded onwards—Te'rnu acting as confidently as he could in the direction he was taking me—until I saw a small maintenance room coming off the corridor to our left. I signalled to Te'rnu, and we crept inside.

'Alright, keep watch,' I told my friend. He manned his post, peering through a small gap in the door.

I looked around the room for the inevitable control panel. On one side, behind the cleaning equipment, I found one.

'Easy peasy,' I muttered, and then hoped I hadn't just jinxed it.

I plugged my console into the panel and ran a scan for accessible systems.

There was only one: emergency exit procedures. A diagram of the building filled the screen, arrows suggesting the fastest way to exit Central Command.

'Shit,' I murmured, and then, realising that maybe I was getting a little carried away with this whole swearing thing, added, 'Excuse my French.'

'What is that?' Te'rnu whispered. 'This... "French"?'

Alright, fair enough—that's a Terran thing, after all.

'It's a dead language, back where I'm from. On Terra.'

'So you were speaking French?'

'Well... no, that's just an expression. It means I said a rude word.'

'Oh,' Te'rnu replied in a hushed voice, 'So the French were a rude people, then?'

I thought about it for a moment; this conversation was going on far too long considering what we were doing, and so an easy answer was required. 'Yes. Very rude.'

I played about with my console some more, hoping I was going to suddenly find some advanced hacking abilities that I never knew I possessed. I had no such luck.

'All I have is emergency exit systems,' I told Te'rnu—and saying this out loud made me realise something. 'But that means I *do* have the building's schematics...'

Te'rnu remained quiet, letting me continue with my train of thought in peace. I tapped frantically at the screen, looking for our destinations.

'...Which means that I can figure out where the core mainframe servers are... And, look! I mean, no, don't look, stay over there and keep watch. But, if you *were* to look, you'd see: there's a room marked 'cells'. Not far from here, either.'

'OK. How far to the mainframe?'

I furrowed my brow. 'Mainframe? Don't you think the *prisoner* is the first priority here?'

Te'rnu whipped his head around to face me. 'Yes. I am sorry. I apologise. I have been searching for the truth for so long... I forget what my priorities should be. We can find the truth later.'

I touched Te'rnu's arm. 'We'll find it. Soon. I promise.'

We proceeded through the corridors and transmats of Central Command through the route I had memorised, me signalling directions to Te'rnu with the smallest of nods. Without running into trouble of any kind, we arrived at the entrance to the cells.

As we walked into the room, a guard, who had been standing almost invisibly still, suddenly stood to attention and saluted Te'rnu.

'Sir!'

Te'rnu was taken aback. '"*Sir*"? Oh! Yes—the disguise!'

Both the guard and I turned to Te'rnu, a look of incredulity on my face (and presumably on the guard's too).

'...mate.'

Te'rnu, realising what he had just said, fumbled his hand around a button by his visor.

'Incapacitate,' I could just about hear the suit's in-built voice announce.

A wave of electricity shot out of the helmet and into the guard, rendering him unconscious.

'Sorry,' Te'rnu mumbled.

I said nothing, only shook my head in exasperation.

'At least we know now what those sparks were doing coming out of the guard's helmet. Back when I stopped you being killed.'

I rolled my eyes, but couldn't help myself from smiling. 'OK, yes, you saved me. Point well made. Let's just not give the game away again, huh?'

I thought that Te'rnu was going to question the phrase "give the game away", but he let it slide this time.

In front of us, next to where the Iyr guard had been standing was a translucent door, an electronic panel to one side. This could only be it—where the prisoner was being kept. I pounded on the glass-like material.

'Hello? Anyone in there? Melonaitopila?' I asked.

Silence.

'If there is... I'm not an Iyr! I'm here to save you! Your dad hired me!' I pleaded.

'...he did?' a voice asked from behind the door. 'Who are you?'

'My name is Syl Raynor. I'm an investigator. We're-'

'Oh!' Te'rnu said, suddenly, 'Why don't we just press this?'

I had only just enough time to shout, 'No!' before Te'rnu selected the "Open Cell Door" option.

'Oh,' Te'rnu replied, 'Why not?'

His question was answered by the alarm springing into life.

Both Te'rnu and I turned to face the door to the corridor, from which direction a stampede of footsteps fast approached.

We glanced at one another, and Te'rnu's hand once again returned to the buttons on his suit's visor.

'Activated: instant kill.'

14. The Diplomat's Daughter

Six Iyr guardsmen stormed the room, all armed with phase rifles—which they promptly pointed at me.

I threw my hands up in the air. 'Alright, don't shoot, I surrender! We don't want an intergalactic incident on our hands, do we?'

The guards suddenly noticed Te'rnu—and all stood to attention. My friend, realising quickly that his cover was still—at the moment, at least—intact, pulled his hand back away from the buttons on his visor.

Quite handy, this disguise.

Te'rnu stood up straight, assuming the role of Iyr Head of Guard. 'Thank you, soldiers, for the reinforcement. I was just in the process of arresting this... intruder.'

He was putting on a lower, deeper tone, pretending as though he had a voice to match his high rank.

'She-,' he began—and then restarted his sentence. 'They already knocked out one of the guards. You!'

Te'rnu pointed at two of the Iyr.

'Take this one to the medical bay.'

'Yes, sir!' the pair responded, and then picked the unconscious Iyr up by their arms and legs.

'That looks comfy,' I murmured, not quite being able to help myself. The remaining guards, enraged by my throwaway comment, picked their phasers up and pointed them at me once again. I was really starting to get used to looking down the barrel of an Iyr phase rifle.

One of the guards slowly moved their hands up to their visor.

'Wait, what are you-' I began to ask.

With the press of a button, bolts of electricity shot out of the Iyr's helmet and into my body, enflaming every nerve in my body, and putting me in excruciating pain.

I screamed like a young child and fell to the floor, barely able to move. The guards approached and grabbed me in much the same way as they had their colleague.

'That's not much fun...,' I mumbled.

Before I knew it, I was thrown into the cell, and the door closed firmly behind me. In one corner of the white, agonizingly-bright room sat a young Itagurinatipilazutinafi woman—Melonaitopila. I forced a reassuring smile in her direction, but in my lingering pain, it came out instead as a distressed snarl.

'Sir, what should we do with the prisoner?' I heard one of the guards ask outside the room.

'I...,' Te'rnu began to reply, 'I will deal with them later.'

Good thinking, Te'rnu. Use your disguise while you still have it.

'Of course—your meeting,' another guard responded. 'It started a few moments ago but I am sure they will understand your delay... given the circumstances.'

'I... err...,' Te'rnu started, stumbling over his response. 'Yes! You: keep guard here. You three, please escort me to the meeting.'

'I do not mean to question your orders, sir, but should we not keep more than one guard on this post, given the security breach?'

'It is all resolved, is it not?' Te'rnu replied. 'The damage has been contained.'

'Of course, sir.'

I heard the whoosh of a door opening and closing, and Te'rnu was gone.

I didn't like that he was out there alone; his cover could get blown at any moment, and I had a feeling I knew what the Iyr would do to him when they found out...

And if he got caught, what hope did I have of escaping?

I turned to the cell's other occupant and flashed another smile at her—which I felt went much more successfully this time.

'How are you feeling?' I asked Melonaitopila.

She looked at me with incredulity, put her hands up in the air as if to say "*what the hell do you think?*"

'Sorry, stupid question,' I followed up.

Melonaitopila shook her head. 'No. It's not. I'm sorry. It's not been a good few days. Or weeks. Hard to tell, from in here.'

'Week and a half, yeah,' I clarified. 'You've been in here all this time?'

She shrugged. 'Pretty much. Since the evening after I saw it.'

'Since you saw the face of an Iyr, you mean?' I asked.

Melonaitopila nodded, her eyebrows twisted. 'How did you know?'

'I told you—I've been investigating,' I replied, and, then, filling the silence that followed, I tried to ask, 'What did you see, Melona- Melonat-,'

'"Mel" is fine,' she offered. '*Any* name would be fine, now, to be honest.'

I flashed her a smile. 'Thanks. Oh! I'm Syl. Guess I should have said that earlier. Getting into bad habits what with never introducing myself properly.'

'Thanks for trying to rescue me, Syl. I'm sorry you got caught.'

'It's OK,' I replied. 'I have a friend. He's... out there, somewhere.'

'Your friend? You think he'll be able to come back for us?'

'I fucking hope so!' I replied—the stigma of swearing be damned.

Fuck! Shit! Crap!

Mel's face twisted into the smallest of smiles. 'You're not like any other Terran I've met.'

'What? Why? Cos I swear?'

'That... and I heard you and your friend assault that guard out there.'

I nodded and pulled an expression that said: "I guess you're right about that."

'Seeing as we might be here a while before Te'rnu comes back...'

'You're sure he will?' Mel repeated.

Why did she keep asking that?

'I'm keeping positive,' I answered. Mel raised an eyebrow again; she was less convinced, it seemed. 'As we might be here a while... now might be a good time to tell me what got you into this mess.'

Mel took a breath and a moment to collect her thoughts. 'I guess there's no harm in it. Not *most* of it, at least. I tried not telling anyone and they *still* locked me up for what I'd seen.'

I held my tongue, resisting the urge to make any facetious comments that might put Mel off confiding in me.

Mel, now beginning to loosen up, began to ramble. 'It started when my father invited me along on his business trip...'

He never invites me to come along with him, you see. But

recently, I've noticed he's started trying to be more involved in my life. I think it's because he's spent most of my life working, and we never really got to be that close. Now he's realised he missed out on my whole childhood, and he's trying to make up for it. I like that he's making an effort, at least.

So, he invites me to come along to Z'h'ar with him. He's got a lot of meetings to go to—because obviously he's so involved with the GMU council and all.

Oh.

Maybe I should have started with that bit. For context.

Yeah, let's rewind.

So, my dad, he wasn't involved much during my childhood because his work at the Galactic Monetary Union Council took up all his time. I don't blame him, really, it's not like it isn't important work. My other dad always called it the "G-MUC" growing up, I remember. Well, no, he called it "that bloody G-MUC", but that's a whole other thing.

In his position, he's involved in negotiating trade deals between planets in the GMU and those outside it. It's a careful balance, he said: you want the trading to be mutually beneficial for all involved, but not so much that these external trade deals are actually better than between GMU members.

He was on your planet, actually, recently. What's it called? Terra? Yeah, when your lot came out of the GMU there was all this stuff to sort out. I didn't see him for a few months during that whole thing. But he did a good job, according to his superiors, and—as is always the case when you do a good job on something—he was given an even more difficult task: Z'h'ar.

Z'h'ar have been talking about leaving the GMU for a few cycles now, especially since Terra came out... OK-ish. So there's been a lot of renegotiations going on, the GMU trying to propose new things to keep the Iyr on board. But it wasn't going well, so, lo and behold, Dad gets roped in.

So we travel over, halfway across the galaxy to come here, and Dad is hoping we will get a little downtime. You know—see the sights, spend some time together.

But... no. It's the same old story as it always was: work needs him, he hopes he'll see me later. I know that that means he will not *see me later. So I have to go out and make my own fun.*

I don't know about for you, but for me, a good night out involves plenty of alcohol and some partying. Oh, right, good, I can see you smiling at that so I know you're the same. You know how it is, then. You get to a new place, you try the local bars, you try the local spirits, you try the... locals.

I was at this bar, and I'm thinking: this isn't quite the scene I was looking for. It's cold, it's awkward, and it's a little bit hostile, even. But I make conversation with this local anyway—he's drinking by himself, so I figure he might want some company. This Iyr, they tell me that these bars are where the Central Command drink, so it's always gonna be not much fun. I ask them to take me somewhere that would be fun, and they do just that.

My date takes me to this underground place, no Central Command, just locals having a good time. I'll tell you what, them having a good time is still quite a quiet night back on Itagurinatipilazutinafi, but at this point, I'm thinking: I'll take what I can get.

I keep drinking, try some of the local Oy'ta—did you try that at all, by the way? No? You haven't missed much. Fairly average. Gave me a nosebleed.

Anyway, all in all, I'm having an OK time, so I invite the Iyr to invite me back to their place. More trouble than it was worth, if I'm honest. We get back there, they take me to bed. I still have no idea what I'm dealing with in the groin area, cos of the mechsuits, you know? But I'm not fussy, I'm happy with anything, so I'm going with the flow.

And I expect my date to actually take the suit off... but they don't. Or, at least, they don't take most of it off. Just the crotch area.

I'm a bit... miffed, but don't want to spoil the mood, so... you know, I guess I go with it.

But then immediately after, the Iyr gets up and heads into their bathroom. I call after them, like, hey, wait, are we gonna, like, cuddle, or what? But they just shake their head and say they need to get my fluids off of them.

Bit rude, I think, but maybe that's just a cultural thing, so I try not to take it to heart.

Anyway, I hear them in the shower and I think: this was all kind of underwhelming, maybe I can get them going again in the shower? Always sounds like a good idea, doesn't it, doing it in the shower, but then you get there and you're doing it, and you're slipping, and...

Doesn't matter, I'm getting distracted.

So I sneak in. And I'm kinda drunk so I'd forgotten the whole "no foreigner has ever seen a naked Iyr" thing. And then, with the door now open, the steam in the bathroom slowly clears... and I see them.

...And that's where this story gets hard to talk about.

What if they're listening?

What if they're just waiting for me to slip up and tell someone the truth?

What if they'll punish me for it?

And all these same questions ran through my mind at the time. When I saw the truth, so much I knew about Z'h'ar suddenly made so much sense... It changed everything. I could see why they'd kept it a secret.

I ran. I was scared what the Iyr would do to me—if it meant they could maintain their rule on this planet. If I told anyone, you see, it could all come crashing down...

I couldn't stay in the stronghold, not any more, so I ran off into the wastelands, to see the only people I thought might understand: the Arellians.

They aren't how the Iyr describe them at all. They're gentle, kind. About as far from "barbarians" as you can imagine. That narrative all makes sense to me now, of course, but...

Anyway. I ran out. Found myself in a village called Te'r'ok, surrounded by these Arellians. And I wanted to tell them the truth, I really did! But... what would I do next? At some point, I had to return to the city—that was the only way home—and if I told the Arellians, I was only damaging my relationship with the Iyr...

I didn't have any option, you see? There was no good choice.

Mel, tired, fed up, and despairing, put her head in her hands.

'What did you see, Mel?' I asked.

'I told you; I don't think I should say.' She nodded to the ceiling. 'Not when they might be watching... listening.'

'We're going to get you out of here, Mel. Te'rnu is gonna come back for us. But we need to know what we're not seeing. We need to know what we're missing.'

'Why do you care so much?' Mel replied. 'Why endanger your own life with the truth?'

I paused for a moment. Was that really what had happened here? Was I risking my life for his truth? Or was I just trying to solve the case? If the two hadn't been so inextricably linked, would I be fighting so hard to learn the secrets of the Iyr?

'My friend... the Arellian, he's spent his whole life searching for this truth. And he doesn't have long left now, he's almost at the age of Mutation.'

Mel shot me a look which I didn't quite understand—*perhaps confusion at the concept?*—but I continued anyway.

'And he's saved me a couple of times now, at great cost to himself. He doesn't have a home any more, he doesn't have a family, he doesn't even have a friend in the galaxy other than me. And, to an extent, I caused all of that. By roping him into some stupid scheme. I think I... owe him this.'

My fellow prisoner looked down at the floor, picked at the skin on her fingers.

'He'll come back for us,' I repeated. 'He's resourceful like that. He'll come back, and we'll get out of here.'

As I said the words, I had less and less faith in them. Te'rnu didn't know the way of the galaxy, so how could he hope to blend in with them? And to get back to us, in the middle of perhaps the most defended building on Z'h'ar... it didn't seem likely.

But I kept this to myself, not wanting to put Mel off telling me the truth. While there was any hope at all that Te'rnu *was* able to come back for us, I wanted to be able to give him the answers he'd spent his whole life searching for.

'OK,' Mel said suddenly. 'I'll tell you. But not because I think he'll come back. I'm sorry, but that's the truth. They're paranoid, the Iyr; his disguise won't last long.'

Mel sighed to herself.

'No. I'll tell you, because, with every hour that passes, I feel less and less confident that I'll ever be free.'

'He'll- he'll come back,' I repeated, voice cracking with the realisation that I might now share the same fate as Mel. This time, I said it only to convince myself.

Mel shot me a sad look.

'The truth is...,' Mel started, eyes glancing towards the door, as though someone was about to burst in and stop her. 'The truth that you've been searching for is... You've seen an Iyr.'

I pulled a face. 'I have?'

'Yes,' Mel replied. 'Anyone who has been out into the Wastelands, or read about Z'h'ar, even, has seen them.'

What?

'What does that...,' I began to ask, and then the truth dawned on me.

'The Iyr—they're no mysterious species, no great benefactors to the lowly Arellians. They *are* the Arellians.'

'Wh- How?' I asked. 'Why?'

'The Arellians don't die when they go through the Mutation. That's not the end of their lives. The Mutation, it's little more than...' Mel paused, to find the right word. 'The closest word we would have for it is... puberty.'

'I don't... I don't understand. Why would they do this? The Iyr—why would they keep the Arellians in the dark about this?'

Mel shrugged. 'It was tradition, probably, to start. All these things start with traditions, don't they? And then you have this society, built up, so reliant on the resources farmed and mined for them by their youth... why would they ever want to change this setup? So they control them. They keep the fear of death hanging over the youths' heads. The Iyr act as though they're doing some great favour when they take a maturing Arellian away—but all they're really doing is adding to their own population.'

I found my mouth hanging agape. 'But that's... that's...'

Mel nodded. 'Maybe now you understand what the Iyr would do to keep this a secret, then. How far they would go. What they would do to anyone who sticks their nose in.'

'But- Te'rnu. He's out there... If he gets found out...'

She nodded again. 'They'll kill him.'

15. A Sheep In Wolf's Clothing

Six of the Iyr guards came into the room, all armed with those horrible phasers. I was beginning to see why Syl did not like them.

The guards, upon seeing Syl, aimed the rifles at her, completely ignoring me.

'Alright, don't shoot, I surrender!' she cried out. 'We don't want an intergalactic incident on our hands, do we?'

At this point, I remembered that I was in disguise. Disguises were good, I had decided. I would have to do disguises more often.

When the Iyr did finally see me, they stood up straight, put their hands to their faces, and shouted, in unison, 'Sir!'

I knew from earlier that this was a sign of respect, that they thought themselves somehow inferior to me (or, at least, to the Iyr that I was disguised as).

Oh! No need for the instant kill, then.

Part of me was disappointed; I wanted to see what it did. The other (much larger) part of me knew that I didn't want to have to live with killing *anyone*—even an Iyr. I pulled my hand away from the buttons on the suit's visor.

I stood up straight, hoping that this was how the Iyr—the so-called "Head of Guard"—would have acted.

'Thank you, soldiers, for the reinforcement,' I told the Iyr, putting on my deepest voice—a mark of authority, I reckoned. And then, realising that I would need to explain this situation in order to keep my cover intact, added, 'I was just in the process of arresting this... intruder.'

The Iyr nodded and remained silent.

Great! I am a convincing Head of Guard! I would never have thought it.

'She...,' I started, pointing at Syl, and then realised that the Iyr did not use that word. 'They already knocked out one of the guards.'

I pointed at two of the Iyr.

'You! Take this one to the medical bay.'

That got rid of two of them. Maybe I should have ordered more away.

'Yes, sir!' the Iyr replied, and picked up the guard I had assaulted by their limbs.

'That looks comfy,' Syl muttered. I tried to shoot her a disapproving look, but it was hard to get the meaning across from under this helmet.

The four remaining Iyr, angered by Syl's characteristically irritating throwaway comments, aimed their rifles at her once again.

I watched in horror, frozen, as one of the guard moved their hand to the buttons in their visor.

Please not Instant Kill!

'Wait,' Syl began, 'What are you-'

When the button was pressed, a huge wave of light came forth from the helmet and shot into Syl, who screamed and collapsed to the floor.

Oops. Perhaps I should have acted sooner there. You need to be better at this, Te'rnu. Oh well. She is still alive. That is what counts!

'...not much fun,' Syl muttered to herself.

The guards picked her up and threw her into the cell, closing the door behind her. I just had a chance to glimpse another occupant, looking tired, dirty, and sad, sat in the corner of that room.

This must be who Syl was looking for.

'Sir, what should we do with the prisoner?' an Iyr asked me.

Think, Te'rnu, think!

'I... I will deal with them later.'

I was going to come back for her later, then. Perhaps in the meanwhile, I could use this disguise to gain access to the central terminal.

But without Syl's technological knowledge...

'Of course—your meeting,' a guard interrupted my train of thought. They looked at a display of some kind on their right arm. 'It started a few moments ago, but I am sure they will understand your delay... given the circumstances.'

Meeting? What sort of meeting? A food-related meeting, I hope.

'I... err...,' I started—and then forced my mouth closed until I could formulate my response properly. 'Yes!'

I pointed to one of the Iyr.

'You. Keep guard here. You three: please escort me to the meeting.'

That should make it easier to break Syl out upon my return.

One of the Iyr turned to me, grabbed me gently by the upper arm. I hoped my biology was not so different from the Iyr that they would notice the difference through the suit.

'I do not mean to question your orders, sir, but should we not keep more than one guard on this post, given the security breach?'

I shook my head. 'It is all resolved, is it not? The damage has been contained.'

There was a short pause.

Had my disguise been seen through?

The Iyr nodded. 'Of course, sir.'

...Apparently not.

One of the other guards opened the door and gestured for me to follow. When it shut once again behind me, it dawned on me that I was alone. I did not have Syl to back me up. I was alone; a Truvet amongst the Hillbeasts, prey in the land of predators.

My newly-formed troupe of guardsman escorted me through the building, along the winding corridors and into the still mind-blowing transmats. In silence, we walked—until, finally, we arrived at a large room.

This atrium was host to a large, long table, at which a number of Iyr sat, each with their suits decorated in their own unique way. If *my* suit belonged to an important Iyr, then these suits did too. Above them was a large, complex metallic web of glass, refracting the light in every which direction. This was art unlike I had ever seen before.

I tried my best not to be distracted by this complicated lighting mechanism—I knew that the real Head of Guard would have seen it many times before—but still it drew my eye. The table turned to watch as I approached the table, and took the last remaining available seat.

As I did so, the Iyr at the very end of the table announced, 'I am glad that we could all make it.'

The table's occupants all looked at me as the room fell silent.

The Iyr across from me but one, with a green upper-half of their helmet, coughed, and then told me, 'That, I believe, was a cue for your to explain the reason for your late arrival.'

'Yes, thank you, Ve'nua,' came a voice from the end of the table.

'Oh!' I said, possibly in a more upbeat manner than was appropriate, 'Yes! There was an intrusion. An off-worlder in the Central Command. It has since been dealt with.'

Many Iyr around the table nodded their agreement. The one at the end of the table, sporting an entirely purple helmet, asked, 'We are not expecting any more intrusions, then, I trust?'

I nodded. 'That is correct.' A pause. I added, '...sir.' It seemed to be the thing to do around here.

'Well, then, as we are not going to be disturbed, may I suggest that we remove our helmets so that we may be comfortable?'

'What?' I found myself asking.

All heads turned to look at me.

'I mean... I am afraid that I cannot... sir.'

'And why not?' the purple-helmeted Iyr asked.

I paused for a moment. It was better to gather my thoughts than to say something that wasn't foolproof. If I got caught, an Arellian, here... then I might not be so lucky as to be let go.

'Because I am the Head of Guard, sir. It is my duty to be ready to fight at a moment's notice. If that means I must be less comfortable, then that is a price I willingly pay.'

Good. That felt good. Very smart thinking, Te'rnu.

A pause. The apparent leader nodded. 'Very honourable.'

Ve'nua continued to stare, even once others had looked away.

Did they see through my disguise?

I felt my forehead begin to sweat and my heart rate start to rise. Was there a mechsuit in this room which could see such things?

I cast my doubts aside; there was something bigger at hand. I was about to see it: the face of the Iyr. Perhaps this would reveal the truth that I had spent my whole life searching for.

I stared at the Iyr leader, whose hands had risen to their helmet, fingers detaching it from the rest of the suit...

My own hands gripped the bottom of my seat in anticipation. *This was it! It was finally happening! It-*

My heart dropped when the first head was revealed. I thought I was imagining what I saw. I blinked over and over as if to wash this hallucination from my sight. But it did not work.

How could this be?

Ve'nua spoke at me. But I could not listen. I could not make out the words.

They paused for a moment and then repeated themselves. This time I could hear them, but as though they were at the end of a long tunnel—only an echo of their voice.

'Are you in full health?' they asked. 'You are acting odd. And your voice...'

'I... I am fine,' I said back to them, with a dismissive motion. They did not seem convinced—but left it at that for now.

As I looked around the room, Arellian after Arellian revealed themselves. I could hear nothing of the debate at the table, only of my own heartbeat. It pounded. Louder and louder it pounded—until my head was filled with nothing but the drums.

How could this be?

I looked again. They were Arellian... but not. Hair sprouted where it should not have. Wrinkles in the skin—like the sort Syl had a few of on her forehead—were pervasive on some of the faces. What had happened to these Arellians to make them this way?

How could this be?

I clenched my hands on my chair. I breathed deeply.

It was almost as though these Arellians were... older.

Ur'tnu had been correct.

He had been correct; we could live on. We could live on past the Mutation. We could live on... here, in the strongholds.

But what would possess these Arellians to abandon their younger selves?

My hearing began to return to me.

'-must be released soon or else we risk war. Is *that* a policy which will aid our economic growth? I think not.'

I looked down the table. An Iyr at the leader's right hand was speaking.

Another interrupted. 'Then what do you suggest? You forget that they are an important person. They are related to the Itagurinatipilazutinafi—the one responsible for our GMU exit deal. If news travels that we have them, here, then what sort of trade deal can we expect in the future?'

They pounded their fist on the table.

'None! We can expect *no* exit deal. All our work over the past three rotations will have been for nothing!'

They look like Arellians, but they do not speak as us. Their nature is that of paranoia, of harm. Who are these Iyr to rule over us?

The original Iyr countered, 'I see that we have two real options. Either we release the prisoner and suffer the consequences, or we keep them where they are until the deal is finalised. As Head of Intergalactic Policy, I favour the former, but-'

'We *release* them? Do you truly understand the implications of this? Not only will there be no deal to speak of, but the truth will be revealed to the Arellians. You are talking about the end of a several thousand-year tradition!'

I noticed Ve'nua still staring at me, seemingly paying less attention to the debate.

A new Iyr spoke up. 'Agreed! The Tradition must be preserved at all costs. Our economy depends on it. If we have no intergalactic trade deal *as well as* no willing manual labour, then we can forget about growth for ten—maybe even hundreds—of rotations!'

Ve'nua, only now looking away from me, spoke up. 'There is… a third option.'

All heads turned to them. There was a silence, even from the leader and their enraged right-hand Iyr.

'They could be disposed of. Quietly. Nobody would ever know that we were involved.'

What? How dare they speak this way—deciding who lives and who dies.

I could feel my heartbeat surging again.

Even the rest of the Iyr remained silent. Equally, however, none immediately voiced an opposition to this idea.

Ve'nua continued, 'What is one life versus the quality of life of our whole civilisation? It is nothing.'

Some of the Iyr began to murmur an agreement.

I tried to keep my breathing consistent, but the anger was limiting my ability to do so.

'You are correct,' another spoke. 'We should dispose of her.'

More murmuring.

Someone thumped the table.

'No!'

I looked around to which attendee had done it.

Strangely, however, everyone was now looking at me.

Oh.

It was… me, who did that.

'Do you have something to add, Pi'nua?' the leader asked.

I paused. Even *I* knew that my pause was for a moment too long. The stare from the suspicious Iyr across the table only confirmed this.

'We are a proud species!' I gambled. 'We have evolved! We no longer need to rely on the... *pathetic* Arellians.'

Was I overdoing it?

With the drums reverberating around my mind, it was hard to sound these sentences out before I committed them to speech.

A pause.

Soon, the leader spoke once more, this time with a tone of resignation. 'Perhaps you are right.'

Still, there was silence from the rest of the table.

'We shall return to this conversation tomorrow. I think there is value in each of us spending the night pondering this issue.'

As they rose, the rest of the table did too. The meeting was over. I had survived it.

I headed for the door—with as much speed as my cover would grant me—and felt Ve'nua's stare follow me as I went.

A clear vision of the next hour formed in my mind. I would break Syl and the prisoner free. We would then, together, broadcast the truth to the world. I resolved to do this, no matter the cost.

The Diary of Leya Raynor

Crowdfunding For Deaths

Gu, 13b-05-2332

So it turned out that the deceased man's daughter, Ti, was still two rotations out; she was taking the *Megashuttle*. This service was, in reality, anything but "mega", and stopped at every so-called planet and ramshackle space station along the way. Clearly, she wasn't earning very much on Rykan. But then, Rykan wasn't the sort of planet you work on if you're trying to get rich. No. It's the sort of planet you work on to have a good time and don't want to faff about with long interview processes. They don't call it the "Party Planet" for nothing.

This meant that I was waiting around with the grieving family for a little while. Over time, I even became quite familiar to many of them—so much so that I became involved in the funeral preparations. To properly understand Gulien funerals (and, therefore, what I was up to over these rotations), you need to know a little history of the planet.

Gu was initially abundant in natural resources—even more so

than most planets. As a result, their economy boomed for hundreds of cycles, and they became a key trading hub for the Iron Sector. Over time, the inhabitants got lazy, began to rely on these natural resources to sustain their wealth, and didn't truly do anything to remedy this situation until the resources were almost completely depleted. By then, of course, it was too late. Surprise, surprise!

So, suddenly everything became unaffordable. People had to adapt, and they started to reuse, recycle, and generally just become less wasteful. But that's not where the problems arose.

The issues came about when all the businesses started to go bust, people lost their jobs, and then income and wealth tax revenues plummeted. Government budgets shrank by over ninety percent in less than one cycle. Suddenly all their services, their programmes, their subsidies and benefits were no longer viable investments. People, now, had to get by on their own.

So death rates spiked for a few years, everyone cut back on having children, people were generally miserable. They have a name for this period in their history... but I don't remember what it is.

[Note to self: look up the name for the period of economic downturn on Gu, and try to remember to edit this bit of the entry later. If you're reading this, and your name is not Leya Raynor, then, whoops, I forgot—sorry.]

I'm not sure any other planet has gone through so much economic turmoil as Gu. Or, at least, there's none that survived it with a written record. But the Guliens did—I guess that speaks to the ingenuity (and, I've come to realise, also the obstinacy) of these people.

So, over time, the Guliens worked out other ways of providing the services that the population needed. Teachers would work for food, clothing, etc from the families of the children they taught.

Guliens sold their bodies for medical testing from trans-galactic corporations so they would cover their healthcare bills. Many emigrated from Gu, and sought out new employment (and new lives) amongst the stars.

You get the idea; people changed. It's funny how there's that old adage that "people don't change". Gu is living proof that they do—when they have to.

Then, somewhere along the way, some Gulien had a bright idea. Out of work and in desperate need of a new shuttle, she reached out to strangers to ask for small donations towards her own personal investment. In return, these strangers would be given advertising space on her shuttle, in proportion to the number of Units they put forward.

The more successful local businesses jumped at the idea. So-and-so's grocery store took a big chunk of the rear. Some mister's tailoring service was plastered over the hoverpads. And the Rykan tourist board, bemused by the idea, paid enough to have the front of the shuttle dedicated to their new spa/hotel complex. (I suspect, perhaps, this wasn't a great move on their part, seeing as most Guliens couldn't afford off-world travel at this point.) Hopefully their ad-man has since found other employment.

The out-of-work Gulien got enough Units for her shuttle, as well as enough to start her own electronics store. It was a rousing success! Hooray! People, both locally and across the globe took notice, and started to draw up their own plans...

So it was then that the Gulien crowdfunding phenomenon began.

The reason all this is relevant is: Gu, still, to this day, does not provide public funeral care. So when this family that I was staying with lost their patriarch, funding became an issue. People emptied out their pockets, looked behind their proverbial sofas, and called up old friends for help. As I suspect is often the case on

Gu, doing all this did not cover the full bill. And, as we know, whenever there's a bill to pay on Gu nowadays... they turn to crowdfunding.

This left a grieving family, sat around their father/brother/uncle's body, wondering how on Gu they were going to come up with a funeral idea novel enough that people across the galaxy would donate to them. At this point, while they were sitting around, having been up all night and craving a cup of U'kka, a stranger knocked on their gate. This stranger, of course, was me.

While I was waiting for the daughter to arrive with the information that I was after, I made myself as useful as possible. There were only so many cups of U'kka that I could make, however, and soon I was roped in to helping in other ways. The family sat me, an unbiased observer, down on the sofa to listen to their various crowdfunding pitches. I (or so they told me) represented the intergalactic community, and therefore if I liked something, there would be enough demand for it to be viable.

The first pitch, from the deceased's two younger brothers, began with a sigh from all the other participants. They weren't happy with this idea, they told me, but the brothers insisted that they were given a fair chance to present their concept.

They began by reminding me of the typical Gulien funeral process; words would be said about the deceased, before the body was covered in a local (highly-flammable) mineral, and set alight. The attendees would typically watch as the fire died out, and once there was nothing but ashes remaining, they would begin to celebrate the deceased's life.

The brother's twist on this would be: they would shoot the body up into the sky, packaged with huge amounts of the mineral, with a short fuse on it. The body, as well as few other explosives, would be set off in the sky, producing a brilliant light show for everyone in the vicinity.

They were perturbed when I said that this reminded me of an old Terran ritual, and when I brought an example of a firework show up on my holodisplay, the novelty of the idea quickly dissipated.

The sister, pitching next, began by playing some soft, gentle Gulien jazz from her console, setting the mood. Her idea, she said, was a classic—and a classic for a reason. She had heard of wealthy people on Terran who seek out and collected chunks of pressurised carbon, which they would often wear on their wrists or around their neck. Her idea was that they would collect the crowdfunding donations as a loan, use these Units to get the body cremated, and then pressurise the remains with overclocked sonar devices. The carbon, she explained, would be pressed into the form that Terrans so often sought out, and so she could sell the remains of the body at a profit. These profits would go back to the crowdfunders, thereby giving them reason to invest.

She was sad to hear me explain that diamonds had long-since gone out of fashion on Terra, and so I wasn't convinced there would be that much of a market any more. Her dejected face made my gut twist with guilt, and I apologised—but she said there was no need. It was better, she figured, that they find that out now rather than later.

Finally, the son, Lo, came to pitch, bringing with him stacks and stacks of something I had barely ever seen before: paper. He dumped it down on the table in front of him and declared that this was his father's life's work. Other families chimed in: he always was a madman, imagine using paper in this day and age, how wasteful, etc etc.

I asked Lo what exactly was written out here, and, more importantly, *why* it was even written out. I was told that it was

163

some kind of medical study—but was largely incomprehensible to him. His sister, when she arrived, would be able to explain more. All that Lo knew, all that he'd ever been told, was that it was important—so important was it, in fact, that his father had refused to digitise it for fear of the information being illegally accessed.

Lo's plan, therefore, was that something kept so secret must inherently be worth something. He would sell this work to the highest bidder; it felt fitting that his father's life's work would pay for his death.

In lieu of any better concepts, it was this last idea that the family agreed upon. The group of us—the grieving family and I— began to scour the pages to try to understand what they contained... and hoped that the sister would bring with her some illuminating knowledge.

It took even longer than expected for the dead man's daughter, Ti, to arrive. Some unexpected meteor shower around Yrgg had meant that the landing queue times grew to over 24 hours, which was particularly frustrating for Ti, considering that she wasn't even getting off there.

Anyway, she remarked when she arrived, she was here now, and they could get on with it. She was a decisive sort—the type of person that everyone listens to when they say something. I think I'm like that a little bit, so we were two like minds.

Ti put the seal of approval on the son's funeral funding plan, and that seemed to be enough for the whole family to commit— except for one of the uncles, who studied her with wary eyes. He was weird, though, so nobody paid him much attention.

Once Ti had put to bed any remaining loose ends, she made some time to speak with me. Lo, Ti and I sat the father's study, and Ti began to explain...

She didn't know exactly what her father's life's work was all about—he really did keep it that hush-hush. But, being only a young child at the time, she had allowed herself to eavesdrop a little. She remembered her father talking to another man about this work, almost as though the other man was in charge. Ti didn't recognise the man at first, but soon became used to him slipping in and out in the night. Once, even, he showed up during the day, and Ti and Lo were allowed to speak with him.

This was where Lo spoke up. This strange man, he was sure, was Ira Raynor, my father. I showed Ti a picture of him, and, although she wasn't completely sure about it, she seemed to agree.

Now that I had confirmation, I pushed Ti on it further. I could taste how close I was to finding him already—and it had only been a few days!

But Ti grew quiet, afraid, and did not like the idea of saying more aloud. Both Lo and I encouraged her to share what she knew, and, eventually, she did give in.

There was one thing she'd overheard my father and her's discuss: telepathy.

Hearing this, all the memories I'd repressed flooded back: the way he'd been able to control me, to control Syl, even.

Of course, none of it was ever done out of malice, or ever intended to cause harm. It was all to protect us. It was to keep us away from potential partners he thought might hurt us. Or it was to keep us inside when the climate was dangerous. Whatever it might have been on that particular occasion, the protection of his daughters was at the heart of it.

But while he thought he was keeping us from harm, we were damaged in a wholly different way. That internal way, that damage to the heart, that might make a mother take 'Liks to forget, or might make a daughter turn to alcohol to suppress her own memories.

At that moment I knew that I needed to own the dead man's work—to understand what its value was to my father.

Although it wasn't quite enough, Ti allowed me to purchase the documents with the contents of my savings. I worried that they'd struggle to send their father off properly if I didn't pay the full amount, but the siblings simply smiled at me. They'd find a way, they told me; Gulians always do.

16. The Truth Is In Here

L eave,' Te'rnu's voice announced from the other side of the cell door. There was a strength in his voice, a determination that I'd never heard from him before.

Come to save my life yet again, you brilliant Arellian!

And then my heart dropped. I realised that—once he broke us free—I would be the one who would have to tell him the truth. A knot formed in my stomach as I imagined breaking the news to him.

'But-,' the guard started.

'Leave. *Now.*'

'Yes, sir.'

The guard stood to attention so hard that I could hear their foot collide with the floor from the next room.

There was a whoosh as the outer door opened, the guard leaving Te'rnu alone in the room.

It was our door, next, that opened.

'I... Mel told me the truth,' I told Te'rnu. 'I know what the Iyr have been hiding. It's... big. I don't really know how to...'

The Arellian remained silent, the mechanic red eyes of the suit bearing into me.

'Do you know already?' I asked.

Te'rnu nodded.

'How? Did you get to the mainframe?'

'I was roped into a meeting.'

'Been there,' I muttered, meaning this throwaway comment to lighten the mood—but my heart wasn't in it.

'We should move. I think one of them is suspicious of me. I know not how much time we have. And there are thoughts of...'

He turned to Mel.

'There are thoughts of killing you.'

Mel gulped. 'Well, I'm keen to get a move on! Shall we go? Let's go. Which way? Left?'

'I know the way,' I told her. 'Follow me.'

We stormed out of the cellblock, Mel and I in front, and Te'rnu holding up the rear, so as to maintain our prisoner-guard dynamic. As we left the room, we turned right... straight into an Iyr.

This Iyr remained quiet for a moment—and looked Mel and I up and down. Their helmet, half the usual dark grey and half green, glistened in the Central Command's neon lighting.

'You,' the strange Iyr commented when they saw Te'rnu. 'What are you doing here?'

'Prisoner transfer,' Te'rnu replied, this strange strength still underlining the tone of his voice. Whatever had happened in the past half hour had changed something inside of him. 'We are taking them to a more secure location.'

'We?' the Iyr asked. 'It looks as though there is only... *one* of you. This is, perhaps, not enough for two prisoners, would you not say?'

'Maybe if it were anyone else, Ve'nua,' Te'rnu responded, and I noted that he was calling them by name—this wasn't their first run-in.

They went quiet; both Iyr staring the other down.

Mel inched closer to me. I felt her gently place something in my hand behind my back. The object felt hard, solid, and round.

Something from the outer cell room?

Ve'nua, currently distracted by Te'rnu, did not seem to notice Mel handing me the object.

Smarter than you look, Mel, I'll give you that.

Ve'nua approached Te'rnu, and stood uncomfortably close to him. They stared into the mechsuit's eyes.

'Is it really you in there?' they asked.

Te'rnu paused for a moment—just very briefly, almost imperceptible to anyone that didn't know him. 'Of course it is.'

Another small silence as the Iyr tried to size Te'rnu up. 'I would like you to prove it.'

'How?' Te'rnu asked.

'Can you two hurry it up?' I interjected, hoping to dissolve the tension. I tapped at my wrist, at an imaginary watch. 'I have a prison to get to.'

Ve'nua turned to me, snarled viciously, and then whipped their head back around to Te'rnu.

'Prove you are who you say you are. Remove your helmet.'

'Ooh, yes please!' I interrupted again. 'I would just *love* to see what kind of body you've got hidden under there.'

Ve'nua turned to me once again and spat their response, 'If you do not keep quiet, I have a function in this suit which will make it impossible for you to be anything but.'

This tactic isn't working. Why do these Iyr have to have absolutely no sense of humour?

I gripped the object in my hand tightly and prepared myself to use it.

'I- I cannot remove my helmet in front of the prisoners,' Te'rnu responded, voice beginning to crack. 'You know this.'

'It is simple: you lock them back up, then you remove your

helmet. If you are who you say you are, you then put the helmet back on, and continue on your way. If you are *not* who you say you are, then I kill the three of you where you stand.'

'I- I-,' Te'rnu began, turning to face me, clearing struggling. 'I-'

I pulled the heavy object around in a flash, and rammed it towards the back of the Iyr's helmet—just as Te'rnu had done to the real Head of Guard earlier. It careered into the small metal box at the bottom of the suit's skull, but—whereas earlier it had caused electricity to envelop the user—nothing happened.

Oh. Not good.

The Iyr froze for a moment, and then, slowly, turned their head to look at me. I didn't need to see a face to know that they were thinking: "Just what the hell do you think you're doing?"

'Syl...,' Mel started, slowly pulling me backwards away from the presumably enraged Iyr.

Te'rnu, in response to my failed attempt to resolve the situation, shot his hand to his helmet, pressing one of those handy function buttons.

An arc of electricity came forth from his suit, and encompassed our troublesome foe. As always, they froze for a moment, their muscles contracting with the voltage shooting through them, and then fell, with a *thud* to the floor.

'You're getting good at that,' I told Te'rnu.

He didn't reply, merely stood and stared at the body on the ground in front of him.

'You OK, bud?' I followed up.

'Are they dead?' Mel asked. ''Cos I would be totally cool with that if he was. I won't tell anyone.'

'No. Just unconscious. Right, Te'rnu?'

There was no immediate answer from him.

'They're just unconscious,' I assured Mel.

I grabbed Ve'nua by the arms, and Te'rnu, without needing instruction, grabbed the legs. We heaved them towards the open cell door.

'Do you always go around knocking people out?' Mel asked.

'Honestly?' I replied. 'More than we should.'

'Cool! Cool energy. Like it! Really like it.'

I raised an eyebrow. *Was this woman OK?*

'Thanks.'

I slammed the 'close door' button on the console and sealed the unconscious Iyr inside.

'OK,' I announced. 'This time, for real: let's get out of here.'

We wasted no more time. I, for one, had no idea how long these Iyr would remain unconscious. Glancing at the time on my console, I could see it had been a good few hours since Te'rnu had defused the situation in the barracks. For all I knew, the real Head of Guard was waking up at this very moment, rushing to the barracks terminal, letting the whole stronghold know what we had done.

We strode with purpose towards the shuttle bay; Mel and I leading the way, Te'rnu at our rear—still acting as though he was transporting us. We walked down countless long corridors, bare in decoration but for the screens every few metres and the small crevices that marked the doorways. As we marched, I noticed more and more Iyr glancing our way—but without being able to see their faces, it was impossible to know for sure what they were thinking.

'Am I being paranoid, or are we getting more looks?' I whispered over my shoulder to Te'rnu, while there was no hostile company in our immediate vicinity.

'I have noticed this too,' he replied, his voice strained, as though speaking through a clenched jaw. 'Do they know?'

I shook my head; the smallest of movements, so nobody else would see that we were communicating. 'If they knew, they would stop us; that suit wouldn't mean shit.'

Mel, in spite of the situation, smiled a little at my response.

'Still laughing at the Terran who swears?' I asked, allowing myself to grin too. If we were about to get caught, there was no point Mel dying miserable.

'A little,' she replied.

As we approached the bay, the screens buzzed into life. I allowed myself a quick glance at them as we strode, and when I saw what they were displaying, I halted instantly. Te'rnu crashed into me from behind, and Mel stopped too, to see what all the commotion was about.

'Oh, my...,' Te'rnu mumbled.

'Understatement of the cycle,' I replied, equally hushed in volume.

On the screen, the Head of Guard—now risen from his enforced power-nap—shouted angrily and impassionately.

We didn't waste any time listening to what he had to say. The jig was up.

'Come on,' I told Te'rnu. 'We're sitting ducks out here.'

'Sitting-' Te'rnu began to ask.

'Come on!' I repeated, moving now towards the shuttle bay with a sprint.

Mel and Te'rnu also picked up the pace, and we charged down the final corridor and into the shuttle bay. We were fortunate that this building was as large as it was—the few Iyr inside could not hope to cover every room.

When Te'rnu, the last to enter, was safely inside the shuttle bay, I closed the door behind him and locked it from the inside— just as a precaution.

I rushed to a nearby docking terminal.

'OK, Mel,' I instructed, trying to make my voice sound as assertive as possible. 'I'm pulling an empty shuttle in for you now. Get on it. It'll take you to the nearest GMU station, and-'

'You aren't coming?' Mel asked, her mouth open with disbelief.

'We're not done here.'

'You've learned the truth! Your job is done! Your debt is paid! They could *kill* you if you stay here!'

I shook my head.

'No.'

'We need to tell my people,' Te'rnu interrupted, talkative again for the first time since he returned to us. 'We can't let them live on like this.'

'You can message them from the station!' Mel pleaded.

'No. The settlement screens are wired into Central Command only. We can't do it off-planet.'

'Te'rnu,' Mel continued to beg, 'Tell her, please. This is *your* fight, not her's!'

'There's more,' I continued, 'There's more I need to do here.'

The shuttle docked and the doors opened behind her.

'What do you need to do? What's so important that's worth risking your *life* for?'

I shook my head. 'There's no time to explain. Get on the shuttle. With any luck... I'll catch up with you.'

Mel went silent, shot me another perplexed face. As she entered the shuttle, I closed the door, but she shot her hand out to stop it.

'Come with,' she said, one last time.

I shook my head, and Mel removed her hand, allowing the door to close. The shuttle undocked and I wondered, for the briefest of moments, whether I would live to see her again.

'Are they outside?' I asked Te'rnu. He looked at me blankly in response.

I rushed over to the security terminal and tapped to bring up the closed-circuit monitoring system.

'They're not. Not yet.'

'OK,' Te'rnu replied. 'Let us take a moment, gather our-'

'No,' I interrupted.

'No?'

'At the moment, they only know that we're in the building. Soon as they see a shuttle leaving the atmosphere, they'll know what *room* we're in. We need to be as far away from here as possible.'

Te'rnu nodded. 'I understand.'

I tapped at the terminal once more, bringing up live feeds to the screens. Tens of Iyr guards filled the images.

Hm. Just how much did I really want this journal decoded?

'It looks as though our path to the mainframe room is clear for now—most the Iyr are at the cells still, retracing our steps.'

'I shall keep my hand on the Incapacitate function.'

We nodded to one another. This was it, then: our big shot.

Te'rnu and I rushed for the doors, sprinting down the corridors that were, according to the screens a few moments earlier, devoid of any enemy presence.

On we ran, fighting our breath as we ploughed down corridors, and praying with every corner that we turned that we weren't about to run into an Iyr—and our almost-certain deaths.

17. Closing In

As we entered the mainframe room, I stopped and turned for one last look. To my disbelief, there was still nobody on our tails. I did some mental maths—we had left the shuttle bay about five minutes ago, and it had taken us the same length of time to get there from the cells. If the Iyr were following in our footsteps, then they were arriving at the shuttle bay at that moment. We didn't have long.

I rushed to the nearest security terminal and tapped to bring up the live feeds once again. I was right—the Iyr were in the shuttle bay already. The Head of Guard pointed at their own security terminal, images of Te'rnu and me on their screens. We couldn't count on having more than a couple of minutes to finish up in here.

'They're coming.'

Te'rnu whipped his head around to look at me, face going white. 'How long?'

'Maybe a hundred seconds.'

Te'rnu nodded. 'I will speak as quickly as I can.'

I rushed to the main terminal, bluffing my way through the user interface until I found the network communications package. As I worked, Te'rnu sat on his shaking hands.

'Do we have time? To decode Leya's journal?'

I glanced at the security terminal. The Iyr were close already, wasting no time in getting here.

I shook my head. 'No. I don't think we do.'

Te'rnu sat aside. 'Go ahead.'

I turned to face him, brow furrowed. 'But if we get caught, your people... they might never learn the truth.'

Te'rnu took my hand and looked into my eyes.

'Syl, if it were not for you, I would never have gotten this far. I would never have learned the truth. You deserve this.'

'No, I-'

'Decode the journal. Then we run. And-'

I interrupted my friend's honourable rambling, exasperated in tone. 'No, stop! *Listen!* We both saw that statue of Leya. We both heard about what she did for Nu'r'ka. She recognised the brilliance, the greatness of your people, Te'rnu. And so do I. Get ready to speak.'

I set the screen ready to record Te'rnu.

'On my mark.'

'On your what?'

'When I say "go", you speak. Tell your whole world the truth. Got it?'

Te'rnu nodded.

I got ready to press the broadcast button, but Te'rnu's hand shot out to stop me.

'Are you sure about this? What if you never find your sister because of this?'

I forced a smile, and it came out sadder than I had intended. 'If I'm gonna find her, I'm gonna find her. We have a saying on Terra: whatever will be, will be.'

Te'rnu returned my smile. His was more sincere than mine was. 'We have that expression here too.'

'Ready?'

He pulled the head off his mechsuit, turned to me, and nodded. 'Thanks, Syl.'

'Go.'

↬

I hurried to the door as Te'rnu began to speak.

'Arellians. Please, listen to me, I don't have much time.'

I poked my head outside and was answered by a wave of phaser fire. I pulled myself quickly back inside, shutting the door firmly behind me.

They were at the end of the corridor already. It was a long way off, but still they would arrive before Te'rnu had a chance to explain himself.

'My name is Te'rnu. I lived in Te'r'ok, just outside the Iyr capital, and I have dedicated my whole life to learning the truth that the Iyr have kept from us for millennia.'

A glowing light appeared in my peripheral vision. I turned to the right to see that the ends of my hair, down by my shoulders, was burning—caught by the phasers. I patted it out as quickly as I could—before any serious harm could come to myself. Unfortunately, serious harm had *already* come to my haircut.

This one's gonna be hard to explain at the hairdresser's.

'I was exiled from my own village for seeking the truth, but now, finally-'

'Hey, Te'rnu?' I called out. 'Might wanna get to the point, buddy!'

My friend turned in his chair to face me. 'Oh! Right! Yes!'

He whizzed back around.

I looked around the room, trying to find some way of getting an advantage over the approaching Iyr. In the corner, I noticed a gun rack—holding only one rifle for the two of us.

'The truth is: the Iyr are not some other species! They are *us*!'

177

I picked the phaser up, held it in my hands... and accidentally fired a beam into the wall.

God, I hate phasers.

Te'rnu instinctively ducked in his chair and turned again to shoot me a confused expression.

I pulled a face in response—and he moved back to the console.

'The Mutation is *not* the end! It is only the beginning! Have you not wondered why the Iyr have always been so keen to help us with it? It is because it marks the beginning of *us* turning into *them!*'

I hurried for the door, and, having learned my lesson, did not peek out for a look. Instead, I held only the phaser outside, shooting beams around the corner—and almost certainly into the wall. I prayed that I didn't hit anyone—killing someone would not go over well with my radical Terran conscience.

'They are using us for their own personal gain! Our tributes to them are the basis for their entire economy! I implore you, all of you, please: stop giving the Iyr anything. They are doing us no favours. Arellians: stand up to them!'

Te'rnu slammed the broadcast button to end the recording and rushed over to help me.

'Quick!' he shouted to me, at a volume I could just about hear over the sound of phaser fire. 'Decode the journal! I will do my best to hold them off.'

Not needing to be convinced, I shoved the phaser into Te'rnu's hands and rushed over to the console, plugging my diary in.

Behind me, the sound of phaser fire quickly faded.

'Err... Syl?' Te'rnu asked. 'I think I have done something wrong.'

I turned to look at my friend to see him pulling the trigger with no effect.

'You've put the safety on! Turn it-'

But it was too late. Te'rnu backed up slowly as a crowd of Iyr entered the room, the Head of Guard at the helm.

Te'rnu and I stepped backwards, away from the Iyr, slowly and cautiously. When my Arellian friend saw that I had raised my hands into the air, he followed suit.

The group stopped a few metres in front of the door, and a silence swept over the room for a few seconds. Tens of red eyes glowed in the dim light, like something out of an old Terran horror movie.

It was the Head of Guard who spoke first, voice swimming with rage, and punctuating each word with a pause.

'You... are... wearing... my... *suit!*' they roared.

Te'rnu gulped.

'Only one of them,' I mumbled, under my breath. Any louder and someone might have heard me.

'What was that?' the Head of Guard snarled at me.

Oops. They still heard me.

'Nothing,' I answered.

The Head of Guard nodded. 'I thought as much.'

At a menacingly slow pace, they approached Te'rnu and me.

'Do you know what you have done?'

I shook my head. Te'rnu nodded.

The intimidating Iyr stopped in front of Te'rnu and held their helmeted face in front of Te'rnu's.

'You have doomed your own planet. Do you realise this?'

'I...,' Te'rnu began to murmur, 'I haven't doomed us. I have told the truth, that is all. We deserve to know.'

'Why? Why on Z'h'ar do you believe that to be the case?' the Head of Guard snapped back at him. 'I was pre-Mutation, once, too, remember. I did my time. Every Iyr in this room did their time. And now that we are old enough to reap the spoils, you do *this*? You cannot possibly imagine the implications this will have.'

The Head of Guard stopped staring Te'rnu down—and moved on to me.

'And *you*,' they growled at me. 'I knew from the moment I saw you in that bar that you were nothing but trouble. This is typical of a Terran. You have been brainwashed by your own people. You subscribe to your own sense of ethics, with no room for any other ideas to be considered.'

They chuckled a resigned laugh. I chose an ashamed grin as an appropriate response.

'No!' the Head of Guard continued, 'Do *not* smile! Do *not* think you have done good here. I will *not* have you thinking this!'

They turned to the group of armed Iyr behind them.

'Guards, ready your weapons.'

I put my arms out in front of me, pleading for them to back off.

'Wait! No! You're really going to kill a tourist?'

I didn't wait for a response; the number of guns pointed towards my face suggested that it wasn't going to be a good one. Instead, I grabbed at my right wrist and activated that ever-trustworthy EMP.

Who needs phasers, anyway?

The *whoomph* echoed around the room as the lights, computer systems, and mechsuits all simultaneously went offline. We were enveloped in almost total darkness—the only source of light being the small window at the end of the corridor.

Without wasting a second, I sprinted towards the door, through the group of frozen Iyr.

'Syl!' a voice called out behind me.

Oops—Te'rnu.

I looked back, over my shoulder, but couldn't make him out in the darkness.

With a sigh, I turned on my heel and rushed back towards him.

'Ah,' I said when I saw him. 'Sorry. Forgot you'd be stuck.'

Te'rnu, like the rest of the Iyr in the room, was wrestling with the hydraulics in his suit—but getting nowhere.

I pulled at the clips around his limbs, one by one, releasing them.

Some of the Iyr guards had managed to move their arms to aim at us, but the *click-click-click* of the triggers suggested that the rifles hadn't rebooted just yet. I knew, at least, that we didn't have long; the phaser in the outpost hadn't taken too long to re-start, and waiting around here for a more precise estimate was perhaps not a great idea.

My friend wriggled free of the last limb—a leg frozen in place on the ground.

'The suits are beginning to reboot already,' Te'rnu told me, voice anxious, 'We don't have long.'

'We don't *need* long,' I assured him.

Te'rnu now free of his suit, we bolted for the door, weaving through the Iyr who were slowly moving to block our exit. We sprinted down the corridor, echoes at our rear of mechsuit feet occasionally hitting the floor as the Iyr trudged on.

We turned the corner at the end of the corridor, heading back the way we'd come—from the shuttle bay. I crashed into an Iyr, who was frozen in place by the rebooting mechsuit.

'There!' they called at another Iyr, standing nearby, equally stuck in their place.

They growled as I picked myself back up to my feet, and joined Te'rnu in continuing our escape.

A phaser beam shot over our heads. The phasers were on back online, then—but at least the Iyr were still struggling to move to aim.

Another shot came—closer this time.

'Te'rnu!' I called out, signalling for him to make a turn.

We shot down another corridor, off to our left.

'We did not come this way?' Te'rnu asked through heavy breaths.

'No,' I replied, equally out of breath. 'But I didn't fancy risking a third shot. I know the way.'

We turned another corner—bringing us back on route to the shuttle bay. In this corridor, fortunately, there were no Iyr to speak of. Perhaps because they were retracing our steps—and we hadn't come this way before.

Soon, the doors to the shuttle bay were back in front of us. Our escape was in sight.

All we needed to do was get in there, barricade the door, and call a shuttle... and then I could get off this damned planet.

We burst through the shuttle bay doors—straight into a squad of armed Iyr guards.

'We thought you would come back this way,' one of them gloated.

18. A Brave New Z'h'ar

I grabbed at the back of Te'rnu's suit, pulling him in the opposite direction, away from the ten or so phaser rifles being pointed our way. We bolted back through the doors... and into yet more Iyr. This was it, then; we were, at last, surrounded—with no more tricks up our sleeves.

Speaking of...

I glanced at the EMP device on my wrist. It was still rebooting, currently up to only 18%.

I looked around for a weapon, for an escape route, for *anything*... but came up empty.

Shooting Te'rnu a sad look, I put my arms up in surrender and slowly returned to the shuttle bay.

The Iyr squad leader gestured towards an empty wall by the door. 'Our boss will want you up against there,' they told us.

Without saying a word to one another, Te'rnu and I walked up to the wall, placed our backs against it, and faced down the group of armed Iyr.

'No,' the same Iyr instructed. 'Face the wall. You will not have the honour of looking your death in the eye.'

Te'rnu slowly turned around to face the wall. I remained still.

'You do not turn around?' the Iyr asked.

I sighed, and in a resigned tone, asked, 'What if I don't? What you gonna do, kill me?'

'Turn around,' the Iyr repeated. I ignored them and instead looked over my shoulder to Te'rnu.

'I'm sorry,' I whispered.

'It is OK,' he replied. 'I think I have done, now, what I was born to do.'

Te'rnu's voice was shaking, and yet his words sounded so confident. He showed strength in the face of death.

Reaching behind me, I gripped his hand, squeezed it gently.

'Turn... around,' the Iyr growled, 'I will not ask again.'

The shuttle bay doors shot open and the Head of Guard stormed inside, followed by the same squad from the mainframe terminal. He took a moment to survey the situation here, before walking up to me.

The red-helmeted Iyr grabbed my right wrist and twisted it so that he could look at the EMP. Upon seeing that it was on only 21%, he nodded.

They looked down at my other hand and snickered.

'Holding hands, are we?' they asked.

I didn't grace them with an answer.

The Head of Guard walked over to the side of armed guard squad, clearing their line of sight.

I glanced at my wrist again: 23%.

'I know what you are thinking,' the Head of Guard continued, 'But that device you have is not going to save you this time. We will be done here long before it re-charges.'

'"Done here"? What exactly does that mean?' I asked. 'You're gonna shoot us? Why?'

The Iyr laughed. '*Why*? You ask *why*?!'

'There's no point harming us now! The damage is done! You're not preventing the truth from getting out there, there's nothing left to hide!'

The Head of Guard said nothing for a moment, and instead simply stared with those mechanical, glowing eyes.

'You are criminals. You *do* realise this, am I correct?'

'Yes, but-,' I started to argue.

'Perhaps I am not correct. Perhaps you think yourselves heroes. This is why your planet has a reputation such as it has, Terran; you believe that your moral compass, your ethics, are absolute. You do not consider, even for a *moment*, that there might be space for different ways of life out here across the galaxy.

'And so, you, safe in the knowledge that nothing you do could be considered evil, head to our planet. You feel free to meddle in things that are *none* of your business. You destroy our way of life, and you justify it to yourself as being the "right thing". Allow me to be the first to tell you this: telling the Arellians the truth about their situation was an *evil* act.'

'How? What "evil" things have I done?'

The Head of Guard raised their voice in response. 'You have destroyed a whole planet's economy! You have doomed countless Iyr to poverty! You have destroyed centuries-old traditions! You have-'

'A good act is still a good act, even if it has *some* negative consequences!' I argued. 'What *evil* thing have I done?'

'Let us see... thievery of Iyr hardware, impersonation of a council official, *assault* of a senior official, fleeing from justice... have I missed anything?'

'Bringing an Arellian into the capital?' another Iyr chimed in.

'Yes! Bringing an Arellian into the capital! That too. Do they really let such crimes go unpunished on Terra?'

'...We believe in rehabilitation,' I replied.

The Head of Guard sighed. 'Of course you do.' They shook their head and then turned to the squad.

'If you're so sure about all this, why are you bothering to debate me? You must know, deep down, that this isn't right?'

'No!' they cried back at me. 'You *must* pay for this!'

'Why?'

They paused again for a moment, and then continued, voice beginning to crack.

'Because... you must! You- you must! You...'

They trailed off, before shaking their head and riling themselves back up again.

'Guards! Ready your weapons!'

Te'rnu closed his eyes, screwed his face up. I looked to him, squeezed his hand, and then turned my attention back to the Iyr.

But it was the contents of the security screens behind them caught my attention.

'Stop!' I shouted, hands outstretched to signal for the Iyr to halt. 'Look at the displays! Look what's happening!'

One of the Iyr turned to look, and then, captivated by what they had seen, nudged their neighbour to look too. One by one, the Iyr all looked over to watch the security screens.

Thousands upon thousands of Arellians marched on the capital, headed for the main gates.

'Sir, we...,' one of the Iyr guards started. 'I think we will be unable to stop them all.'

'Guards!' the Iyr group's red-helmeted leader shouted. 'Back to your post! Raise your weapons!'

'But, sir...,' another piped up. 'Look.'

Another member of the squad started tapping frantically at the security terminal. 'Sir! It's not just here... it's the whole planet.'

'Raise your weapons!' the Head of Guard repeated, voice beginning to falter. The Iyr didn't move, still transfixed by the marching Arellians on the monitors.

'Come on, mate, don't you see?' I asked. 'It's over.'

'You don't need to do this,' Te'rnu offered. 'Z'h'ar is changing. It is happening before our very eyes. Whatever world we had yesterday will be gone by tomorrow. Whatever rules you think you have to follow... they'll be gone too.'

'He's a smart one, really, isn't he? Don't you think it's time to let it go?'

Our foe sighed—and remained still for a moment before reaching their arm up to their helmet.

'No, don't!' I called out, wincing in anticipation of the weapon feature that I believed was to come.

But instead of pressing one of their helmet's buttons, they began to remove it. Beneath it was an Arellian, but unlike I had ever seen before. This one had more striking features, a slimmer face, and bright green beautiful eyes.

'Perhaps... you are right,' they mumbled.

One of the Iyr guards noticed that their leader had removed their helmet, and followed suit. And after a few seconds, more Iyr noticed, and more. Soon, all the Iyr in the room had revealed their true face, and then those outside the room followed suit.

The Head of Guard turned to me and forced a reluctant smile. 'I guess, perhaps, it is time.'

All of us—the Iyr, the Terran, and young Te'rnu—spent a few moments standing in silence as we watched the Arellian horde filter in through the main gates and spill out into the streets. There was a certain sense of beauty to it; being here as an entire population grew into themselves, as a whole world changed.

When the sheer awe began to wear off, the Head of Guard silently gestured for the Iyr to follow them. Soon, it was only Te'rnu and I left alone in the shuttle bay, the changing Z'h'ar displayed on the security screens around us.

The hums of the building's generators and the slight buzzes from the displays filled my ears. They seemed to grow louder with every moment that I spent in this room, perhaps even on this planet.

'Te'rnu, I... I think it's time for me to go,' I whispered, nodding to the doorway. 'In case they change their minds.'

'You don't want to see how this all turns out?' he asked.

I shook my head. 'I know how it goes. The exploited people rise up against their exploiters. They demand reform. The exploiters give it to them—because they're outnumbered. Things... get better. It takes time, but overall... eventually... it gets better.'

'This happened on Terra?'

'More times than I can count.'

We fell into silence. I ambled over to the shuttle terminal, glancing at the door to check that no Iyr were watching me, that none were ready to change their minds, pounce, arrest me for my supposed crimes.

'Where will you go?' my friend asked.

'First thing I'll do is go see Mel. Make sure she got out OK. But then, after that, I'll go wherever they send me.'

'Who?'

'My agency. There will be another case. Not as exciting as this one, I'm sure, but it'll pay the bills. Maybe some quiet job would be nice after all this.'

Te'rnu went quiet, began to stare at his feet.

'What is it?' I prompted him.

'Can I come?' he asked. 'Can I come with you?'

I furrowed my brow. 'Te'rnu... this is your home here. Are you sure you want to leave? Just as things might finally get better?'

He shrugged. 'I did what I had always hoped to do. I don't know what I would do here, now. And I am not sure it is my home any more. I cannot return to Te'r'ok, my real home, and... I am not sure I would recognise it after all this. My real home truly does not exist any more.'

I paused for a moment to gather my thoughts and then pressed a button to summon a transport ship.

'But what would you do for work? It's expensive out there, and...'

'I have some ideas,' Te'rnu replied, a sly grin on his face. 'May I come?'

'Te'rnu... I mean... the whole point of... of *all of this* is that you can do whatever you want! If you want to get on this ship then that's up to you. You don't need my permission—or anyone's, in fact.'

He nodded to himself. '...I guess so.'

The docking port opened with a whoosh, the transport ship having locked in outside.

'Time to choose, Te'rnu. What'll it be?'

He stood still, frozen to the spot.

I walked onto the ship, staring at him from across the threshold.

'What do *you* think I should do, Syl?'

I shook my head. 'I think it's your decision. I can't help you.'

There were a few more moments of silence. Te'rnu looked up at me, eyes wide.

'Will you still...,' he began, before trailing off.

'What is it?'

'Will you still be my friend? Out there?'

I laughed. 'Of course I will, mate. Whether you stay or go, I'll be your friend.'

Te'rnu nodded; one firm, confident motion. 'OK.'

He stepped onto the ship.

'Glad to have you aboard, Te'rnu.'

We sat down in the shuttle's cockpit and I programmed in a

189

route for the nearest station—where Mel was hopefully twiddling her fingers in anticipation of my arrival.

'Is it scary?' Te'rnu asked.

'Is what scary?'

'Flying through the stars.'

I shrugged. 'Not sure; maybe I've just gotten used to it.'

I started the engines, and Te'rnu's eyes widened with horror. He gripped the seat firmly as we shot out into the atmosphere, and then, when it all became too much to handle, scrunched up his eyes.

'Yeah, I guess I've just gotten used to it, then.'

I left him to it for a while, keeping an eye on my watch to see how long it would take him to calm down. In the meantime, I tapped at my console, hoping to get a message through to Mel; but the station was too far away, there was too much interference. In fact, *everything* was too far away from this damned planet.

There being nothing I could do for the moment, I took a few minutes to take the time to centre myself. The last few days had caused my muscles to tighten, my neck to ache, and there was this slight thudding pain in my temples. I closed my eyes, concentrated on my breathing, and before long, I had drifted off to sleep.

'Are you awake, Syl?' Te'rnu asked, the sound of his voice bringing me to.

'Yeah...,' I mumbled. 'I guess so.'

'I don't see anything. Is that normal? It is all so... dark.'

'Yeah, it's normal,' I replied, words still slurring slightly as I awoke.

'But there are so many stars out here,' Te'rnu continued. 'So I thought it would be bright.'

'There's nothing for the light to bounce off, though.'

'What do you mean?'

I shook my head, rubbed the sleep from my eyes. 'I'll explain another time.'

We sat still, staring out into the darkness, the lights from the control panel in front of us illuminating our faces in eerie shades of reds and blues. I looked down to notice that my jacket had been draped over me like a blanket. I shot Te'rnu a smile, but he didn't see—instead, he stared out at the empty spacescape, transfixed by the great beautiful nothing.

I became conscious of stiffness in my legs from being cramped up in this spacecraft for however many hours it had been. I stood up, touched my toes a few times, and began to wander the ship— not that the ship was really more than one small room.

Te'rnu looked around and watched me.

I ran my hand across the edge of the ship, feeling every crevice. I soon came to a small U'kka dispenser, with long boxes of spare parts at its base.

'You had U'kka before?' I called out to Te'rnu.

'No?' he replied.

I pressed a button on the machine—but was presented with an error.

Faulty hardware. Please call a technician.

I sighed. 'Maybe that's for the best.' I could picture Te'rnu after getting a caffeine fix and the idea filled me with terror.

I next found myself in front of a storage container, running from the floor to the ceiling, about the same size as me. Unable to resist the temptation, I pressed the button on the control panel to open it up.

The cupboard whirred into life, the front folding away, and the interior repositioning to properly display its contents: a mechsuit.

'Hey, Te'rnu,' I called out. 'Have a look at this.'

The mechsuit in front of me was decorated with a thick purple stripe, running diagonally across the body from the left shoulder to the right hip.

Te'rnu arrived at my side.

'Looks like the Iyr have left you with a little gift.'

'I am not sure that was their intention,' he replied. His hands reached out to gently touch the suit.

'Maybe not. But maybe you *should* be given one. You know… for services to your people.'

'Do people get gifts for that?' he asked.

'They do on Terra. Well, they used to give *titles* rather than actual objects, but I think this is better in your case. Try it on!'

Te'rnu needed no further prompting—and stepped forward into the suit. It instantly came into life and adapted to his form, with all those satisfying whirring noises that accompanied such mechanical genius.

'How's it fit?' I asked him.

'It is…,' he began, fumbling for the buttons on his helmet, but not finding any. Looking down at his arms, however, he noticed some, and pressed at a button. The helmet unfolded from his head, retreating back into the body of the suit. 'It is good! Better than a title, I think, too.'

I laughed. 'We shall see. Get on your knees.'

Te'rnu narrowed his eyes. 'Why?'

'Terran thing. Just do it.'

Reluctantly, he got to his knees. I picked up one of the longer boxes from in front of the broken U'kka dispenser, and tapped Te'rnu on either shoulder.

'When you rise, you shall rise as Sir Te'rnu, knight of Z'h'ar!'

He looked up and broke into a wide grin. 'Knight of Z'h'ar! I like that.'

'Better than the mechsuit?'

'Not quite. Sorry.'

I snickered again. 'Fair enough.'

The control panel at the front of the ship beeped. Ahead, sparkling in the distance, our destination was just about in sight.

Epilogue

We collected Mel and landed on Itagurinatipilaz, where her father welcomed us. Mel explained to him—sparing absolutely no detail, and going off on a lot of tangents along the way—how we'd been the ones to save her. Her father responded, in turn, by hugging each of us for several minutes. He was so happy, in fact, that Te'rnu and I each were left with a wet patch on our shoulders from where the tears of joy had flowed.

We were hosted by his family for several days, each day treated to new feasts, activities, and everything else that the planet had to offer. If solving *every* case had been rewarded like this one was, I might have tried harder in my work.

On our second day on Itagurinatipilaz, Mel, Te'rnu and I were given, free of charge, access to the planet's premier spa. While Mel and I gushed in agreement that this was exactly what we both needed after everything we'd been through, Te'rnu tried to eat every product the attendants put on his face.

Leave the cucumbers alone, Te'rnu.

Between treatments, I received a message on the console from my mother which made my gut twist in horror. The communication, with no signs that she was speaking ironically or that she was under duress, told me that she was proud of me. When I replied, pressing her on this further, it turned out that our rescue of Mel had made galactic news—even if it was a little overshadowed by the revolution on Z'h'ar.

If I had felt any joy in reading those messages from my mother, it was whipped away from me when a second communication came in—from Saotchun.

I groaned audibly as I realised that it was from him. Te'rnu's face shot up from a mud bath when he heard this.

As always, I skimmed the agency message.

...where the hell are you? We have people ringing for you! Jobs to be done! ... Heard about the bonus that the client sent you. Regulations stress that such bonuses must be paid directly to the employer, a.k.a. me. ... I expect the units to be deposited by ... If you wish to continue with your employment here at this renowned agency, you shall respond within ...

I huffed and sighed as I skimmed it, and suddenly realised that Te'rnu was reading it over my shoulder.

'This is your new boss?' he asked me.

I rolled my eyes and nodded. ''Fraid so.'

'I... have an idea.'

I turned to face him properly. 'What is it?'

'Do you remember when I boarded the ship for the first time? And you asked me what I would do out here amongst the stars?'

'Yeah...'

'I could work for you.'

I moved to speak, but Te'rnu interrupted me before I could.

'Let me finish, please! I could work for you, and *you* could be the boss. I know you were sent a reward for your work. Do not give it to this... *Saotchun*. Use that to start your own agency, where you can take the cases *you* want, and where you get to take the rewards for yourself. You do not need to work for these people.

You are smart. You are capable. I know this.'

'And... you would work for me?'

'Yes,' Te'rnu replied, nodding. 'You would teach me. I would be your assistant. If that would be OK with you, that is.'

'I don't know, Te'rnu... starting a new business, it's difficult, and it's hard to find new work and get off the ground, and...'

'I read that message, Syl. There are people calling for you, this Saotchun says. I know that I know little of the galaxy, but my understanding is that there will be no shortage of work out there.'

I considered this for a moment. Deep down, I knew there was only one real answer:

Fuck it.

'OK.'

Te'rnu's eyes widened. 'OK? You will do it?'

'Yes,' I replied, watching as a smile took over Te'rnu's face. 'But we only take cases that will help people, if we can. Deal?'

'Yes! Deal. I agree,' Te'rnu replied. 'And...'

'And what, Te'rnu?'

'I know you were not able to decode all of Leya's journal. But we have a part of it. We can take jobs on planets that we know she visited. We can learn more. Perhaps we can decode more, too. Maybe we will even find her along the way.'

I found my mouth stretching into a smile. 'Yeah. Maybe we will.'

A GALAXY, ALIVE
CONTINUES...

in

A PLANET
THAT
LONGS
TO
FORGET

Read on for a taste of what's to come

1. Raynor Investigations

Him!' Solita shouted, pointing at an Abinaxian who had just turned the corner into the shuttle terminal. Her voice carried, alerting my target to our presence. Looking over, he saw Solita - my informant - gesturing towards him, and immediately began to sprint away.

'Cheers,' I said to Solita, both sincere and insincere in nature; she might have led me to my target, but she also got him sprinting away from me.

I don't appreciate having to work for my fee, thank you very much.

At least I had planned for such a scenario.

After I charged out the shuttle terminal in pursuit of the fleeing local, I spotted him in the distance - crossing the station square. I weaved between shuttles as I crossed the road, causing their emergency brakes to automatically kick in, and resulting in a chorus of complaints from their passengers.

I'm doing this for your own good, idiots!

My console *ding*ed with notifications as the inconvenienced locals left negative reviews on my Abinaxian Network profile.

Distracted by my depreciating Abinaxian standing, I tripped at the curb of the road, staggering for a moment before catching myself. I clambered upright and continued running. The ground squelched beneath my feet as I trampled what must be the only green area for kilometres around - the station square being the minimum requirement of parkland in urban areas as prescribed by the GMU.

In the distance, the suspect was fast approaching my first planned obstacle. The road ahead was completely blocked off, ribbons and crowds stretched across the walkways to mark the perimeter of the all-important *Abinaxian of the Year* awards. Well, maybe not so important - it was only the first rounds, after all.

The target, realising his mistake, darted right, leading him across the edge of the square. Perfect! I hadn't planned for him to go left here - although that would have put him on the main road, which would take some amazing feat of agility to cross unscathed.

'Approaching reroute point number two,' I breathed into the console on my wrist.

'Copy. Roger. Over,' that familiar voice replied.

I jumped off the grass, onto the main walkway at the edge of the square, and, looking ahead, found that I was only 100 metres behind the target.

Maybe we won't need that second obstacle after all.

I ploughed onwards, threading through the crowd of commuters that were heading for the shuttle terminal for their journeys home. My smaller form made this easier for me; I could slip through the smallest of gaps, whereas, up ahead, the suspect bumped shoulders with those around him, slowing him down.

As I gained on him, I began to hear the growing commotion. Commuters grunted at the barging man, while he himself seemed to be getting more impatient with those getting in his way. Voices ahead began to shout, but still the suspect continued onwards.

The suspect was fast approaching the end of the street - and obstacle number two - while I was only a few metres behind him. I reached my arm forwards, hoping to catch at the back of his jacket - although the chances of that stopping him were slim to none.

I snatched at the cloth, missing it by mere centimetres at this point - when the suspect turned the corner.

'Wham!' shouted Te'rnu, as he stepped out from behind his pre-determined hiding spot. He collided with the suspect, and, with the strength of the mechsuit backing him up, stood still standing, while the suspect fell to the ground.

'Wham?'

'Yes, you know: *wham!*' Te'rnu replied, folding down his helmet to reveal his smiling face. 'Like the sound that nice coyote makes when he runs into those tunnels he draws for that bird. You know, the one in the Terran shows. This is like that: *wham!*'

I said nothing for a moment, so he continued.

'In this instance, I am the tunnel, and our suspect is the coyote.'

'We really need to get you some more up-to-date references,' I replied.

At our feet, the target began to scramble away. 'Shall I...,' Te'rnu began.

I nodded, knowing exactly to what he was referring. 'Go on then.'

Te'rnu pressed at a button on his mechsuited wrist, and bolts of electricity shot from it into the escaping suspect, incapacitating him.

I pressed at my own wrist, too - but where Te'rnu had cool mechsuit functionalities, I had only my console. I sent my drafted message through to the local police, telling them that we had successfully apprehended the target.

'Let's see if you've got any of it on you,' I murmured as I

crouched down by our horizontal suspect. I patted him down and found - to no surprise whatsoever - that he did indeed have some of the Stirlik needles on him.

I looked up at Te'rnu. 'Hey, you're recording this, right? I don't want there to be any doubt that these weren't planted on him.'

Te'rnu nodded.

'I suspect some of our competitors out there would plant stuff like this to get paid...'

The local police soon arrived - a local Abinaxian who seemed more preoccupied in smiling at passers-by than she did at handling our apprehended suspect. She nodded to us, and then, eventually, scanned the man that I was holding to the floor.

'Ha. No wonder he's a criminal,' the police officer said. 'Look at this.'

She turned her wrist to show me the information on her own console.

'...Only thirty followers,' she continued. 'Surprised he didn't resort to a life of crime earlier.'

I laughed along, pretending as though my own social media profile had more than twelve followers - among them, an overprotective mother, an employee who only recently left the village he grew up in, and a sister who had been missing for several years. Te'rnu knew enough to keep his mouth shut about this.

'Will you have enough to prosecute him with?' I asked. 'Given that there's a chance that his buyers won't have any memory of him any more.'

'I think you overestimate him,' the police officer replied. 'Low-follows like him don't usually have the brains it would take to program the 'Liks in that way. I suspect those memories will be undamaged.'

I shrugged. 'OK. Cool. Anything else you need?'

The officer shook her head. 'Nope, all set - I'll take him in. Thanks for your help with this. I'll give you a 5-star rating.'

I shrugged. 'No worries. I mean, we're getting paid for this, not like we were just doing it out of the kindness of our hearts.'

'Four stars, then, maybe,' the police officer replied, before hauling the suspect into their van.

'Maybe you should have-' Te'rnu began, but then I nodded to show that I had realised my mistake there.

Small footsteps patted the ground behind us, and I turned to see Solita, our informant, running to catch us up.

'I see you caught him. I guess your client will be happy?'

She patted me on the arm as if to say *"good work"*.

A headache came over me, and I blinked back the pain from the momentary searing pain.

Fuck, that's come on quick. Must be the hangover kicking in.

'Well, that's what you get when you hire the best detective agency in the galaxy,' I replied, forcing a smile through the pain.

'I am not sure about that,' Te'rnu contradicted me. 'By no metric are we the best; we do not bill the most, we do not have the highest rated reviews, we do not-'

'Yes! Thanks, Te'rnu,' I replied.

Solita approached Te'rnu, patted him on the upper back. 'Oh, I'm sure you're better than you think,' she told him. 'You caught a 'Lik smuggler, after all. No easy feat.'

We soon parted ways, and Te'rnu and I headed back to the shuttle station - for transport off this planet. A big part of me was glad to see the back of it.

↲

Once settled in our off-world shuttle, I began working on writing up a report for the client. This was my least favourite part of the job, but I couldn't yet trust Te'rnu to describe the nuances of our work correctly. That is to say: his reports made our work sound too easy, and perhaps not worth the amount we were charging our clients. I, on the other hand, enjoyed buying expensive things and running a profitable agency, so I tended to employ artistic license when writing up the reports that we sent with the invoice.

After this case, however, I had another reason to play fast and loose with the truth: I couldn't quite remember everything we'd done. It was those damn famous Abinaxian cocktails that had done it - how could anyone say no to them? There were cocktails that changed flavour as you drank them. Some fizzed and popped and even buzzed in your mouth. Their most famous cocktail of all was known as Liquid Fire - very literally, an alcoholic plasma which warmed you as it poured down your throat. It was this drink, in particular, that meant my memory was a little fuzzy, my throat a little sore and my head a little achy.

Te'rnu glanced over, eyes narrowed, as I tapped furiously at my console, keen to wrap up the report so I could relax for the remainder of the journey. My friend's angry eyes were not enough to make me type more quietly, and he was far too polite and proper to speak up about it.

'Told you we don't need a team,' I announced to Te'rnu as I sent off the final report and invoice - without, admittedly, spending the time to read it back to myself.

Te'rnu shot me a look which roughly translated to: "I don't agree but I don't want to have this debate again". If he were Terran, he would have rolled his eyes in a big, big way.

Not minutes after I sent the report and invoice, the client contacted me. In fact, when accounting for the amount of time it would have taken for the signal to reach her, it was more like seconds. My console beeped to let me know that a communication was coming in.

I breathed a heavy sigh; a response this quick could only mean that the client was going to push back on the amount we were charging. I put myself into sales mode before answering.

'Hello?' I began, 'I mean- Raynor Investigations, Syl Raynor speaking. How may I help you?'

'Syl! Hi!' the client responded. 'I just got your message. I wanted to check that I'm understanding this right - you've finished the job already?'

Oh! It was going to be the opposite problem, then - not having charged enough.

'That's right, Huara. All sorted. Got the distributer, all locked up now, I believe. Shouldn't be any more 'Liks on Abinax any time soon.'

'Oh, really?' the Huara replied. 'As easy as that?'

'As easy as that,' I reiterated.

'I thought it would take at least a few weeks. Well... I guess I'm not complaining - means you're charging less, after all.'

Damn it, I really should have stretched this case out a little more.

'I mean... yeah. I guess we are. I sent my report along with the invoice - if you want to give it a read and then you can give me a buzz if there's any questions?'

'I'll do that!' Huara replied, and the line went dead.

'Well... bye, then,' I muttered pointlessly into the headpiece.

The call over with, I turned to smile smugly at Te'rnu.

'Easy as pie,' I said.

'"Easy as-",' he began to question, then changed his line of enquiry. 'Do you remember...'

'Remember what?'

Te'rnu's brow was furrowed. 'Do you remember how we knew that suspect was the one we wanted? It's a bit of a blur to me.'

'You got a headache, mate?' I asked, pointing at the pained

expression on his face.

'Yes, I guess that I do,' he replied.

I held a finger in the air - *one moment* - and reached into my bag, pulling from it a bottle of aspirin.

I threw the bottle towards him. Te'rnu caught it, opened it, and lobbed a couple of tablets into his mouth.

'This will help?'

'Usually helps me,' I replied, noting that my head, too, was hurting - that hangover not yet having loosened its grasp on me.

'Ah,' said Te'rnu, pointedly, 'Yes. Of course it does.'

If you're gonna call me out on the drinking, Te'rnu, just go ahead and do it.

'I think...,' Te'rnu began, his eyes widening. 'I think this might be...'

'Iyrogenesis?' I asked.

He nodded.

'Well... let me know if the pain gets worse. Chances are it's just a headache, though. We all get them - no need to get ahead of yourself.'

'Not me,' he murmured, and then sat back in his seat, strikingly still.

I checked the time left on our journey - still another good few hours. Not quite enough time for a good sleep, but certainly enough time to make a cup of tea or two.

Standing from the seat, I made my way over to the dispenser and programmed in my order.

'Want one?' I called over to Te'rnu.

'No...,' he replied, still not moving.

'How's that head? Getting better?' I walked over to his seat and stood over him.

'I think so.'

'Good,' I replied - and patted him gently on the shoulder. 'No transformation for you just yet, then.'

The shuttle console beeped - we'd been assigned a landing time. There would be no queues on Terra today, not this once.

I sighed, sat back down in my seat. It was time to spend the remaining journey preparing myself - both mentally and emotionally - to once again face the single biggest challenge I had in my life: my mother.

This time, at least, I wasn't alone.

Head over to ReyMorfin.com to sign up to the newsletter and be alerted when new books get released!